MELANIE SILGARDO was born in the University of Bombay, and publishing house, Newground London where she worked for several years at Virago Press as a commissioning editor. She co-edited *Virago New Poets* (1993), has taught creative writing at the Arvon Foundation, and is one of the judges of the 1996 Saga Prize.

Short Circuits

·

Twelve New Writers

·

Edited by Melanie Silgardo

A *Virago* Book

First published by Virago Press 1996

This collection and introduction
copyright © Melanie Silgardo 1996
Copyright © in each contribution held by the author

The moral right of the author has been asserted

A CIP catalogue record for this book
is available from the British Library

ISBN 1 85381 868 2

Typeset in Times by M Rules
Printed and bound in Great Britain by
Clays Ltd, St Ives plc

Virago
A Division of
Little, Brown and Company (UK)
Brettenham House
Lancaster Place
London WC2E 7EN

EDITOR'S NOTE

Short Circuits emerged from the need to provide a conduit for the volume of new fiction by unpublished writers that arrived with frustrating regularity on Virago's slush pile. Two years ago *Virago New Poets* was published for the same reason. No profits were made, every last copy was sold, and a little hope was introduced into the equation.

When I invited contributions for *Short Circuits* through literary journals and magazines, and the happy conspiracy of writers' workshops and groups, I was flooded with responses. Just administrating the pile was frightening. Then came the really hard work of reading, assessing and eliminating. It was a slow and arduous process. I tried to make my selection as democratically as I possibly could. I even stopped myself reading the biographical notes that accompanied each batch of stories – the pressure to find young and/or ethnically/culturally various writers plagues the editor more and more. I wasn't looking for equal representation, just fine stories.

Twelve writers stood out, writers who were attentive to

their craft and to their voice. Writers who were exploring uncomfortable territories – the brittle and tenuous connections with family, the darker regions of sexuality, the night-terrors of childhood, the spectres of old age and death. Universals, inspected with such remarkable acuity of vision that I was truly excited. I wasn't looking for a unifying theme but one emerged – each story meeting the next at a tangent or crossing it, forming a kind of complex circuitry.

Two of the writers here have novels coming out almost simultaneously with this collection. Others who've never had their work in print suddenly find their work included in other anthologies as well. For them, and all new writers, I hope that publishers will continue to provide space such as this so that new writing can continue to flourish.

I'd like to thank Virago for the generosity, despite hard times, that made *Short Circuits* possible; and much thanks to Sia Smyth, Helena Anderson and Kasha Dalal for all help.

Melanie Silgardo
London, 1996

CONTENTS

Georgie's Girls

·

MIRIAM BURKE

After work, the lads and I go back to the flat and get ready to go clubbing. There are three of us who work together and share a flat. Georgie lives there too, it's his flat. We fight about who gets into the shower first and sometimes we all get in together. There's lots of shrieking as we help each other decide what to wear. I usually go for a loose linen jacket, a silk shirt and baggy trousers. The flat is in Mayfair and it's heavenly. Louis Quatorze repro furniture and water-beds. We have a cleaner, a sweet Malaysian boy, who comes in every day. We got his residency sorted out through a lawyer client of ours. He likes to be called Maria.

We drop a tab of E before we go out and open a bottle of Veuve Cliquot. There are always bets on who's going to score. We jump into the 'bus' – Georgie's black convertible BMW. He keeps it in the basement garage space that comes with the flat. If we knock off early enough we go to a nou-velle cuisine restaurant for a nibble. The E doesn't take hold if you eat too much. Then we buck about the town like pucks who've just had their ropes cut. We take a few snorts of coke to give an edge to the E mellow, and pocket some amyl nitrate in the hope of a score. Georgie plays Callas singing 'Un bel di' as we drive to the clubs, and we all sing along.

We do about four clubs a night. I like the one that isn't too queeny. The one with the married men. And the politicians who have orgasms at the prospect of being caught. Navvies hungry for the tenderness they can't accept from a woman. Elderly judges and barristers staring out from the shadows, with a fear that is too old a friend to leave them now. We're known wherever we go. They call us 'Georgie's Girls'. If we don't score, we go for a walk by the river, or in a park at dawn. The E takes you that way. And afterwards, we often go to a cafe to ogle at the workmen. We've been in a few scraps, I can tell you. Then it's back home. We usually sleep in each other's beds, flopped on top of each other like a litter of pups.

Maria wakes us at midday with large Bloody Marys. I approach the Bloody Mary the way I approached the porridge all those mornings long ago. 'It'll fortify you Liam,' my mother used to say. We squeal over the tabloids for a while, have a snort of coke, and it's down to Old Compton Street for lunch. We have a table permanently reserved, so everyone knows where to find us. People come to join us or just stand and gossip for a few minutes. We set off to work about half four. We get the punters on their way home from the office.

We fall in love every year or two, but Georgie doesn't panic. Some hunk with a good job takes one of us to live in

Hampstead or Chiswick. It's a dream for a few weeks. Shopping together in Sainsbury, walks in the park, cuddling in front of the video. I've now learned to split before the Semtex ignites. I'm having a very nice time with a lovely man and suddenly I explode. It seems the happier I am, the worse the rage. I scream vicious, unforgivable things, smash his favourite things, and often land a punch or two. It's back to Mayfair and we all have a good laugh about it. Georgie doesn't even bother to get someone to cover my pitch any more, I'm never away for long enough.

Sometimes we go to the more specialised clubs. I needed hospital treatment recently, after a particularly wild night in one of them. It was in one of these clubs that I thought I saw him once. Big fat fucker that he is. I can always tell a priest. The combination of the haircut, the flabbiness, and the underwear. I was eight when he suddenly started coming around to the house, having cups of tea with Mam. I suppose she was lonely and the fucker knew it. My father always seemed to be at the dogs or playing cards. He'd often be coming home as I was going off to school. Anyway, Father Mick brought up the issue of me becoming an altar-boy. And hinted to Mam that maybe I could go on to be a priest. She was thrilled with that, of course. She had no great regard for the sacrament of marriage after her own experience of it. And the thought of me looking after her in her old age, in the way a priest would have to, was very appealing. She fantasised about the ordination in the way another mother would about her daughter's wedding. So I started serving Mass in my red cassock with the white starched surplice. I'd look at his back as he raised the chalice and my small body shook

• 5 •

with hatred. I'd always hated him, funny isn't it.

I was a happy lad. Mam used to make a great fuss of me because, I suppose, there was no one else to fuss over. The other lads liked me because I was funny. Although small and thin I didn't get bullied because I was smart. They knew I could make a laughing stock of a lad, if I had a mind to. I loved English and always got top marks for my compositions. I could tell Dad was proud of me. He'd always introduce me to his friends when I bumped into him coming out of the betting office. It was a great town for a boy to grow up in. We'd spend the summers fishing and larking about in the river or riding bareback on donkeys all day in the woods, our small boys' eyes dazzled by the creatures there.

I think Mam was a bit in love with Father Mick. He had clean fingernails and soft hands. The rough country ways get knocked out of them in the seminary. And she could confide in him about my father. He'd spend hours listening to her when I was at school. There were no jobs to be had in the town, and there wasn't much housework with just the three of us, and one of us never there. She'd come from prosperous people and married my father against the wishes of her people. We had no contact with them. My father, and all belonging to him, were work-shy. Nice people, but work wasn't in their blood. So she had the worry of him out of work most of the time. She did some dressmaking to support us.

Father Mick had been coming around for about a year when he started to horseplay with me. He'd push me to the floor and then wrestle with me. Mam would look on pleased, thinking that's how a father should be with his son. I'd feel sick. Then he asked me to stay late after Mass to help him put things away. He'd send the other altar-boy home. If I got stuck taking my cassock off he'd rush to help me, his hands lingering. It was a Sunday in November. I knew from meeting him in the sacristy before Mass that he was in a wild mood. He rushed through the Mass. He attacked me as soon as the other altar-boy had left. He still had his vestments on. He pushed me up against the wall and rammed it in. Jesus, it hurt.

I walked slowly home, I could feel the blood and semen hardening. She knew something had happened when she saw me. I said I was sick and asked if I could go to bed. The bastard came around after he had eaten the big Sunday dinner his housekeeper always made him. She left him alone with me. He said that if I ever told anyone he would have me sent to an industrial school where it would happen to me every day.

I kept getting sick when I ate and I couldn't sleep, so she kept me off school for a few days. Every time I closed my eyes I would see him coming towards me. When I went back to school, everything was different. I couldn't take in any of the lessons. My mind was out of focus. And I couldn't do my homework because I was always listening for his knock on the door. In the end-of-term exams I got the lowest mark for English. The English teacher spoke to my mother and said that whatever was happening to me, it was a terrible shame. He said he had had great hopes for me. He thought I'd be a journalist or a writer. He offered to provide extra coaching after school. I was too frightened to go.

I started to hang out with the wild lads in the town. We were always in trouble, stealing and fighting. I must have got some comfort from it. I gave her hell at home. I'd do nothing she ever told me to do and as soon as I was big enough I hit her. After that I ran riot. At fifteen I ran away and came to London. Georgie spotted me at Euston Station early one winter's morning. He said he had a flat he needed some honest Irish lad to look after. His mother was from Tipperary, he said.

We haven't been tested, but we've all got it. We don't even use condoms unless they insist. I refuse to go to any more funerals. At first, we got hysterical if any of us caught a cold, but we're cool about it now. We could run for another ten years. They might even find a cure, and then what would we do? We'd be too old for this lark. What else is there for us? A council flat, waiting for the giro. So really it's just as well.

I have a cockney accent now. It used to drive me mad: 'What part of Ireland are you from? Do you know so and so?', they'd say to me as I stuck it in them. I'm from the town that produces rent for the export market. And yes, I knew Father Mick, a great man. He's a Bishop now isn't he? I bet he looks good in the purple socks.

The lads are very amused by my 'special' condoms. I always carry one packet of johnnies that are far too small. Not that I'm that big. I suppose they're for teenagers or tourists from countries where they're not so big. As soon as I spot the short hair and the flabbiness, I'm in there like a shot. If I'm working, I offer to do it for half the normal rate. They love to think they're getting a bargain. As it bursts, I come and shout, 'Take that Father'. And I watch him walk slowly away, infected by fear.

P i g l a d y

·

CHARLOTTE PRICE

'If you notice, most folks . . . go to church only when they've got to; but a hog is different.'

Mark Twain, *The Adventures of Huckleberry Finn*

The week Muriel visited her grandmother in Darlingham, she spent her allowance on the Bible verse that went, 'With your gear you shall have a spike, and when you have squatted you shall dig a hole with it and cover up your excrement.' Pammy Miller, her grandmother's eight-year-old neighbour, sold it to her for twenty-five cents.

It was a good one, Muriel agreed, worth every penny. Deep in the woods the girls sang a scatological song called 'Deuteronomy' and squatted under a tree, underpants at their ankles, trowel at the ready. But the moment Muriel stood up,

Pammy stopped grunting, unpuffed her cheeks, and relaxed the tendons in her neck.

'I guess I don't have to go after all,' she shrugged. And holding her nose, she came to inspect the knobbly brown corn-cob lying at Muriel's feet.

Afterwards, Muriel struggled up the path behind her, leaves crumbling under her sneakers, underpants damp with drops of urine. Pammy chanted:

> Milk,
> milk,
> lem-mon-nade,
> 'round the corner
> *fudge* is made!

Pointing to her nipples, her groin, her pink-culotted candy-factory of a derriere. Then she added, 'I'm telling your grandma what you did!' and charged up the hill.

'*Grand-ma . . . !* Grand-ma . . . *! !*' whispered the birch trees along the path.

Once in Art, Muriel had carved eyes and a nose from a peeled Macintosh apple and set it on the window-sill to dry. Six weeks later, shrunk to half its original size and rubbery with wrinkles, it looked so much like her grandmother she got scared and hid it under the radiator.

'I don't *want* to go to Grandma's,' she had wailed as her mother dug through the piles of old newspapers and mis-matched boots at the bottom of the hall closet. 'She *picks* on me.'

But when her mother emerged, grim-lipped, with a duffel

bag smelling of cat pee, Muriel saw it was no use. Something had come up, something unexplained.

'I know, Muriel,' her mother had said. 'I just don't see any other way. Try to remember it's only five days.'

So far, Muriel had survived three of them by never gulping her milk and dabbing at the corners of her mouth whenever her grandmother did. All that morning she'd been almost happy: only two more days to go.

'*And now Pammy Miller's going to ruin everything!*' hissed the weeping willow at the edge of the lawn.

Muriel veered round the corner just in time to see the little brass hoofshaped door knocker fall from Pammy's hand with a clatter. The door opened and Muriel's grandmother appeared. Beaming.

'Pammy *dar*ling!'

Pammy dropped the curtsey she'd perfected in gymnastics.

'Well, if you aren't the *cunningest* little – Muriel, isn't Pammy the cunningest –'

But she broke off mid-sentence at the sight of her granddaughter's hair, a clump of which had escaped from one of her braids and was plastered to her sweaty forehead.

'What on earth's happened to you?'

Nothing, Muriel knew, provoked her grandmother like long hair. That morning she had clamped her between her knees and, with her thousand-toothed comb, raked two crooked braids from the weeds. 'All this *hair*,' she had said. The way someone else might have said '*phlegm*'.

Now with a sigh, she lowered herself on to a lawn-chair and turned back to Pammy.

'*Someone's* been to the beauty parlour, I see.'

Pammy nodded, curls rippling like eel grass in the wind, and without skipping a beat, said, 'Muriel helped me choose the Bible verse I'm going to write my Sunday-school report on.'

'She did? Well, isn't that too good to be true. Why just this morning she refused to go to Mass. "I don't believe in God," she said. I had to leave her outside!'

In the field next to the church had been a blue and white tent crowded with people: the 4-H fair. While Muriel stood behind a pole, waiting for her grandmother to come out, a man had hung a blue ribbon around a sow's neck. The runners-up hurtled about like bumper cars, and Muriel thought she had never seen pigs so naked. Pink and oily and bump bump bump. Naked as a squeal.

'Which verse did you pick?' her grandmother asked Pammy now.

But Pammy ducked behind the lawn-chair, pulling at the corners of her eyes until they were two slits. 'Confucius say: he who fart in church sit in own pew,' she whispered, just out of Muriel's grandmother's hearing aid.

'Which one, dear?'

Grinning, Pammy did a pirouette.

'*You* tell her, Muriel!'

Then from next door, a wind-chime of a voice tinkled: 'Paaamela, luuunch!'

But Muriel wasn't out of the woods yet.

'Walk me half-way home,' Pammy ordered. At the end of the driveway she began to chant again: 'I'm telling my mo-ther. I'm telling my mo-ther.'

Muriel splashed the rubber tip of her sneaker through the tiny white pebbles. 'Don't. OK?'

Pammy said, 'OK. How 'bout I tell her you're from the planet your-*anus* instead?' And she was so inspired by the idea she dashed across the lawn and did a perfect handstand.

'Hey, Muriel, what's brown and sounds like a bell?' she croaked, culottes bunching up around her scissoring thighs.

'I dunno,' Muriel answered, on the verge of tears.

'*Dung*!'

From the lawn-chair, Muriel's grandmother watched Pammy cartwheel home. 'Send my love to Big Pam!'

Nicknames were rife in Darlingham. Pammy Miller's mother, though she was renowned for the precision of her bone-structure and took a size petite dress, had been called 'Big Pam' ever since the birth of her daughter. And Muriel's grandmother had been 'DD' since 'the beginning of time'. (Though, if pressed, she would recount the story of the admirer who had coined the phrase 'Doyenne of Darlingham' one riotous evening.)

DD collected admirers and in turn, her admirers collected pigs. Not for themselves; as gifts for her. No one knew how it all started. But whatever the origin, all of Darlingham agreed it was a kick, seeing the porcine offerings DD's devotees brought back from around the world to lay at her shrine. Big Pam was proud to have given her the very best pig in her collection: an apron with pigs' heads for pockets, on which she'd embroidered 'Our Darling Ham!' across the chest. DD wore it on Thursday evenings – Cook's Day Off – to poach her egg.

'I think of you as a second daughter,' DD had written at the end of her thank-you note. She didn't put in the part about her own daughter, Elizabeth, always making a mess of things, but she didn't have to; Big Pam knew all about it. Elizabeth had left Darlingham when she was eighteen, in the same pair of stockings she'd worn every day for a year, sealing up the runs with Cherry Shudder nail polish until her legs were puckered with acrylic scabs. Things had been difficult between them ever since.

Big Pam had a chorus line of 'Oh dears!' ready to prance out every time DD told the story of her visit to Elizabeth's first apartment in New York: it was a tenement in the West Forties (oh dear); Elizabeth shared it with a 'Semitic-looking man' (oh dear) – *whom* she eventually married (oh *dear*); after all, it was many years ago, before DD knew what to make of such things (of *course*); and DD had almost put her foot through a hole in the living-room floor (oh *no*!). Fifteen years later, DD still shuddered when she thought of the bundles of wire and coils of copper tubing she had glimpsed through that hole. How like Elizabeth to refuse to have it repaired, leaving the very bowels of the building exposed.

As for her granddaughter, DD told Big Pam she was exhausted by Muriel's manners at their occasional Sunday lunches, and by Elizabeth, ready to bite off her head if she so much as *mentioned* an incorrectly held fork. Let alone Muriel's religious education. At her progressive school they had replaced the Christmas pageant with a celebration of the winter solstice. 'If you ask me,' DD confided to her neighbour, '"progressive" is just another word for "pagan".'

It was during the tea-break at the Christ Church Ladies'

Liturgical Committee meeting that Elizabeth had called to say she needed DD to take Muriel for five days.

'But it's the middle of the school year!' Big Pam said when she heard.

DD lowered her chin and raised her eyebrows, her not-in-front-of-the-other-committee-members look.

'Well, Pammy and Muriel will finally have a chance to get acquainted,' Big Pam said, eye to the bright side.

'It *would* be marvellous if Pammy's manners rubbed off a bit,' DD had agreed doubtfully. 'Muriel's are the absolute bottom.'

On the fourth morning – one more to go! – Muriel was sent into the bathroom with its orange-sherbet walls, while DD did her telephoning. She sat on the closed toilet seat, gazing at the shelf where the best pigs were kept, until it was time to flush, then poked her head into her grandmother's bedroom.

'Hold on a moment, Big Pam.' DD held the receiver against her hip.

'Grandma, I don't have to go.'

'Well try.' And she went back to her phone call.

Under the sink was a footstool. Muriel pulled it over to the shelf and brushed her finger across the Indian pig in the lotus position and the felt pig in a plaid waistcoat you could unbutton. At the end of the shelf was a sad-eyed sow on a celestial-blue cushion, with eight piglets suckling at her porcelain teats. Muriel had just slipped the runt in her pocket when she heard her grandmother say, 'But they don't have two cents to scrape together. How on earth could they *afford* a second child?'

There was a pause.

'Of course I offered to help, but her analyst says she's in no emotional state to go through with it.'

Another pause, in which it occurred to Muriel the sow's teats were like her grandmother's bosoms. Sad sacks that swung when she hoisted her spotted leg immodestly over the side of the tub and lowered her bottom into the steam. They pointed down, like arrows to the ground.

On the other side of the door her grandmother said, 'Well, they're this generation's priests, I suppose. Oh, isn't it just like Elizabeth to get herself into this mess.'

Muriel put the piglet back on its cushion and jumped off the footstool. Hearing the toilet flush a second time, DD told Big Pam Muriel would *love* to have supper with Pammy, of course, and hurried off the phone. She found Muriel crumpled on the floor, hugging her knees to her chest and had to call Big Pam to say Muriel had a stomach ache and wouldn't be at supper after all.

At seven a.m. the morning of the fifth day, Muriel woke up in the blue-painted guest room. While she was studying the profusion of monogrammed blanket covers, pillows, and bed spreads on the other twin bed, in order to better reassemble her own, the cook tiptoed in. Her grandmother had had a heart attack and been taken to the hospital in the middle of the night, she informed Muriel. Breakfast was ready and her mother would be there shortly. Sure enough, Elizabeth arrived just as Muriel was sliding her overcooked egg into the kitchen-table drawer. They would be staying, she explained, looking exhausted, until she had managed to confer with the doctors and arrange for full-time nursing care.

The next day, Big Pam made her first and last sortie into occupied territory. Armed with sympathy and a devilled-crab casserole, she found Muriel arranging pigs in rows around the baby grand, and Elizabeth, still in her nightgown at two in the afternoon.

'*Your* mother . . .' Big Pam sobbed with careful emphasis.

Elizabeth's expression was inscrutable. 'Yes. My mother.'

When the pigs were seated, Muriel bowed from the piano bench, and raised her middle finger. But the first note of 'Heart and Soul' was a dud. Elizabeth helped her lift the back of the piano and they found a dozen stuffed pigs inside.

'Fecund little creatures,' Elizabeth smiled, turning back to Big Pam. 'But then, my analyst says the pig was once worshipped because it was such a terrific breeder. That and the fact its snout looks like a plow . . . Rooting about in the muck – you know the way they do.'

Being with Elizabeth was like being hissed at by a cat, Big Pam told the Liturgical Ladies afterwards. She would have kept her distance even if Pammy's upcoming gymnastics meet *hadn't* required her to spend all her free time at the gym.

It would be brief, Elizabeth explained after her meeting with the surgeon, and DD, preferring to die in her own bed, was coming home.

'But don't expect her to be the same. This has aged her twenty years.'

Muriel was waiting at the front door when they drove up.

'Hateful place, heaven,' DD muttered as Elizabeth eased her over the threshold.

'You mean the hospital, mother.' But this only seemed to confuse her more.

Later, when Elizabeth was going over dietary restrictions with the cook, DD managed to extricate herself from the sheets, but told Muriel she would need a hand getting to the bathroom.

'I'll just get Mom,' Muriel said, looking away from the twisted-up nightie. But DD said, '*Now*.'

'I kept thinking the whole time I was in that awful place,' she mused as Muriel lowered her on to the toilet, 'that it isn't language or religion which separates us from the animals. It's that we leave such a mess behind us when we go. No other creature burdens its relatives so.'

She was tiny sitting there, a shrunken apple bobbing about in a sea of blue satin and lace. But the finger she pointed at the inflatable pig in the window was formidable as ever.

'Muriel, dear, deflate that thing.'

The rush of air as the pig collapsed around Muriel's fist echoed DD's own triumphant fart.

'Well,' she sighed, 'that's *something* anyway.'

The funeral took place on the day of Pammy's meet. Muriel spotted her in her pink leotard and tutu, glowering at Big Pam two rows back.

From somewhere above them, bells sounded the beginning of mass: *Dung*. Muriel and Elizabeth sat as the congregation formed a line, shuffling past the choir stalls to the altar. Pammy placed her right heel exactly in front of her left toes, then repeated the whole thing in reverse, practising her balance beam routine.

'Well, if that Pammy Miller isn't just as *cunning* as ever,' Elizabeth whispered. Muriel smiled and touched her cheek to her mother's shoulder.

'I miss Grandma more than I thought,' she said.

'She was a tough old bitch,' Elizabeth agreed, blowing her nose into a crumbling Kleenex.

When the Eucharist was over, the congregation knelt to give thanks. Muriel closed her eyes, trying to imagine God so she could tell Him her grandmother wasn't as bad as she seemed, but before she could get Him clearly in focus, she was interrupted by a loud *PSSST!* When she opened her eyes, there was DD herself, floating on a light-blue cloud, just above the crucifix. A litter of ladies, whom Muriel recognised as the deceased members of the Liturgical Committee – though they looked far better-fed and more serene than they ever had in life – were curled up beside her, fast asleep.

'Are you OK, Grandma?' Muriel asked silently.

'OK?' shouted DD, 'I'M HAPPY AS A PIG IN SHIT!' And disappeared.

'Good-bye,' whispered Muriel.

The members of the congregation struggled up from their prayer-cushions and opened their hymnals. Tall and twiggy and tuneless as trees, they joined their voices together: the celebratory hymn.

Suddenly, the carved wooden doors swung open behind

them and sunlight stormed into Christ Church. The sound of hoofs, then a spotted pig, two-hundred-and-fifty pounds of pork and a wet shiny nose the size of one of DD's demi-tasse saucers, emerged snorting from the tunnel of light. It pounded down the aisle, nipples swinging, stopping every few steps to hurl its snout into one air current or another.

A lady-like scream went up. Husbands reached protective arms around their wives, and children hid between their mothers' knees.

The pig took a sharp right into the pew where a quivering Pammy Miller had wedged herself as far as possible into a corner, and truffled its wet nose under her skirt.

Big Pam whacked it with her purse, but it was no use.

It had found the bottom of its dreams.

C r y s t a l
B a l l

.

HELENA ECHLIN

They are late. Kate seethes with irritation. She is doing Granny a big favour by taking her to church, so the least she could do is be on time. Especially tonight, Christmas Eve, which she had been planning to spend with Richard.

A young man ushers them to a pew when there is a suitable pause in the speaking. Kate shrinks as Granny's bulk squeezes past the other worshippers. She won't even sit still. 'Oh, I can't seem to get comfortable,' she whispers loudly, fidgeting like an ancient cat, turning round and round before it sits down. As usual, she has plumped down uncomfortably close to Kate. Kate slides away, pretending to be adjusting her position on the wooden seat. Is it her imagination or is Granny inching after her? The camel coat is pressed against her. Warmth seeps through it. Strange, Kate did not expect her to feel warm. She never thinks of there being a body underneath all those layers of clothes, the jumpers, cardigans and coat. She imagines the clothes going all the way down, a cloth body, like a rag doll. Or even one of those mummies in cartoons, the kind where you unwind all those layers of bandages to find nothing underneath. She edges away again, imperceptibly. She just needs to have a space between them, even a few centimetres. It's the physical contact she can't stand.

The smell is stronger than ever in the chilly air of the church. It's the scent of old-fashioned pink or white soap, the kind with the brand name engraved on it that comes in white wrappers with pictures on: roses, angels, babies. In Kate's mind religion has this smell, this insinuating sweetness, with a faint, rank trace of something else underneath.

'And here's Kate,' cries Granny obviously, just arrived for her Christmas visit. 'I must say, you're looking quite the young lady now.' Kate wishes she were still young enough to be able to shy away from the wet kiss imprinted on her cheek. The kiss on meeting and parting is the only time any of the family ever touch Granny, as far as they can help it. No one can have touched Granny for years and years, she ponders. If, or possibly when, that happens to Kate, she will feel numb from the neck down, as if she is only a head. Perhaps her grandmother is hardly aware of her body's existence any more. Unable to remember what it looks like, seeing nothing but layers of clothes when she looks down.

The numbers on the hymn board remind Kate of a doctor's waiting room, or else the job centre. There is the same sense of expectancy, of awaiting possibly unpleasant revelations. Guilt nags at her. She thinks at any moment they will all stand up and start loudly, joyfully, confessing their sins, or else a long arm will point at her from the pulpit. She never liked going to the kind of shows where they pick people out from the audience.

The priest's voice goes on and on. Kate can shut it out just enough so that she can hear a drone but no words, like hearing the news going on in the next room. Granny does not even look that interested. The expression on her face is meek and blank. Kate supposes she must feel a sense of duty fulfilled. She is not fanatical about her religion, just dogged. Every birthday Kate gets a crucifix.

The first was a delicate little silver one, but they have become progressively, defiantly, larger. The most recent was made of chunky pottery, edged with gilt and painted with a Biblical scene, flat amazed faces looking skywards. Kate imagines them peering in dismay at her unbelieving head above them, poking through the heavy chain. She thinks it is as if Granny thinks the granddaughter she rarely sees is growing indefinitely into a giant, needing larger crosses, her vast face receding into the sky. Or perhaps she wants Kate to be weighted down, to stagger under them as a reminder. To bear her crosses. Next time, jokes Kate wryly, the cross will be full-size, two planks at angles, nailed fiercely together.

In between birthdays Kate gets cards with scalloped edges and illuminated borders saying: 'The monks of St Ignatius' monastery are praying for you', or 'The sisters of the Convent of the Sacred Heart remember you in their prayers'. These go straight in the bin. She doesn't like the thought of other people interfering in the future of her soul, if she has one. She doubts this, but the cards chill her all the same.

Occasionally there is a whole booklet, warning her to repent and be saved. This can be done, she is informed, by reciting the following: 'Dear Heavenly Father, I respond to your invitation and come to you in the name of your Son Jesus Christ'. Short at least. The prayer is on a pink background and reminds Kate of the tear-off response to party invitations she got as a child. At the end of the booklet there is a blank postcard saying: 'YES! I have been saved! Please send me more literature on the Christian life'.

Her grandmother always has some little gift to offer. However unwelcome. Once it was home-made marmalade that had failed to turn to jelly; thick amber liquid like ancient home-brewed wine, like jars and jars of cod-liver oil. At Christmas it is always a cake. Kate's mother tells her every year on the phone not to bring one, but every year she manages to forget this polite refusal. 'You can't do all that stirring with your arthritis, Mum,' Kate hears her mother saying. The words are solicitous but the tone warning. Nevertheless, Granny struggles under the cake's weight, cradling it on the long train ride up to London. The cakes are symbolic, like all Granny's cooking, not intended for eating. As winter softens into spring the cake lies at the end of the garden, untouched even by the squirrels. It's like a small meteor dropped there, heavy and solid.

Granny staggers into the house and stands there, hugging the cake, bemused, as if she is not sure what it is or why she brought it. As if, in a passing clouding of her mind, she'd picked up a rock to take with her by mistake. Grainy, crumbling rock, sedimentary, the kind made of different stones stuck together with sand, raisins encrusting the outside like black diamonds. Pebble-dash, like her house, as if she is bringing it to them, chunk by chunk. Kate's mother says Granny would like to move in with them. The cakes are evidence of pain, they are reproaches. All that stirring and stirring in the tiny kitchen, forcing the spoon through the thickening concrete mixture. Stirring, which is also the word Kate's mother uses for starting an argument, sends spasms through her wrist. Kate wonders what she thinks about when she's doing it. Kate would think about Richard.

Kate cannot imagine what goes on in her grandmother's mind. That she once had a boyfriend too, and later a husband, is inconceivable. Her hair has always been white, her eyes watery faded blue. What does she look like? Kate can hardly remember. Is it that her face is so familiar it has become invisible? The eyes are always blurred by the large glasses, as if she is floating underwater. Maybe Kate has never really allowed herself to see it; she shrinks from doing so. The lipstick is vivid though, the greasy mouth chewing at meals till only a fuchsia outline is left. This is all she can recall without looking: outlines, wavering and dissolving. Every old woman she passes could be her grandmother. After a certain age they all become the same woman, a fuzzy shape rubbed out and redrawn a great many times.

Mabel, May, Doris. Lumpy beige tights and bright, bright pink lipstick. But when Kate is old her name, so fashionable now, will be a name that only old ladies have, and she'll be wearing the colour of lipstick she's wearing tonight. She touches her face in fear.

Granny is standing up. It is time to sing. Kate always

feels embarrassed to sing when she's standing next to some-one she knows. Granny comes out with a cracked quaver, like an old gramophone. Perhaps because they are tucked away in a pew to the side, perhaps because they are pressed together sharing a hymn book, it seems to Kate as if they are singing alone, their voices swelling out with increasing courage.

On the television a model appears, holding a perfect, shining apple. 'But *this* is what can happen if your skin doesn't get enough moisture,' says a voice. 'Can happen', as if wrinkling can be completely avoided rather than just postponed. They would never show an old woman, age can only be approached symbolically. An apple filling the whole screen quickly puckers and sags. 'You massage the cream into your face like this,' says Granny, kneading her neck and cheeks. 'I used to do those kind of things, but at my age I don't bother. There's no point.' She is living evidence that these creams can't put it off for ever. Her skin looks too soft, over-kneaded, loose and stretchy like an old balloon. Kate has a momentary picture of Granny gradually deflating, collapsing. She must care about her appearance then. She notices for the first time that the white hair is permed.

Kate and Richard decide to introduce him to Granny for a joke. She doesn't know why this prospect excites them. Perhaps it is the thrill of shocking her. Perhaps she and Richard like the old-fashioned formality of it, as if he was her fiancé meeting the family for the first time. She wonders how Granny will take it. She has no idea what her moral stance on boyfriends is. Nevertheless, when Kate and Richard wake up in Kate's bed, Richard creeps downstairs and rings the doorbell, pretending to have come round that morning. 'Oh, hi Richard! Come in,' calls Kate loudly. She is annoyed, she can't give a natural performance with him crumpled up with laughter in front of her. Besides, she is uncomfortable about giggling helplessly in front of Granny. Though the old lady seems so meek, so blind. 'My eyes are weak,' she says. 'You'll have to speak up, dear. I'm getting rather deaf.' Kate feels she and Richard could get undressed and Granny would just carry on with her embroidery. She seems to miss so many double-edged comments. Or maybe that's what you do with sarcasm, shut it out and pretend not to hear.

'That is a nice young man you've got there,' Granny says to Kate later. 'I've had a few proposals in my time, mind you. They always used to be pestering me, in fact. I remember one of them was an architect, although I couldn't fancy him personally. "If I can't marry you," he said, "I'll never have anyone else." Then straight after that he proposed to a little bit of a thing from the farm up the road and now they're living in a huge house on the downs. I always think that could have been me living in that house . . .' The voice talks incessantly, a long, soggy string being pulled on and on, out of her throat. 'Um,' says Kate. 'Ah. Oh really.' She hasn't got the energy to vary her responses more than this, but Granny doesn't seem to notice. She seems compelled to unburden herself, like the Ancient Mariner. Kate wonders why she is being told about these past proposals. Maybe at her age Granny is haunted by the sense of other lives she might have had, ghost lives running parallel to hers. Maybe she is trying to tell Kate that she too was once young and desired. Kate sees the shape of a young girl outlined in Granny, floating in cloudiness like a plant frozen in ice. She looks in the mirror and sees round herself the shape of an old woman, nebulous now, but gradually solidifying.

'Has Richard rung you yet, dear?' Kate cares about this more than she thought she would. 'Don't worry. Give them forty-eight hours, that's what I always used to say. You'll have many more such disappointments.' Kate's mother would think this callous, but Kate thinks Granny is only trying to warn her. She senses some stifled longing in the old woman, the fingers of a young girl struggling to reach out and touch her through the flesh.

But she can't help it, she can't help recoiling. She doesn't want these confidences, this weight of longing. Grandmothers should not have past lives, they should be born old. 'Have a sweet, dear,' whispers Granny, surreptitiously holding out a crumpled paper bag. 'No thank-you,' shudders Kate. She knows about the emotional significance of food. To feed someone is a way of binding them to you. Granny is always giving her sweets, as if she were still a child; old-fashioned ones, too brightly chemical for Kate: liquorice allsorts, dolly mixture, jellybeans. This is what her love is like, too sweet, overpowering, poisonous. Any moment now, thinks Kate, the cup will be held to her lips, the wafer placed on her reluctant tongue.

Adroitly, Kate manages to get in front of her in the queue. She doesn't want to drink from the cup after Granny. As

Kate kneels she notices the little Nativity scene they've set up. The Virgin is clutching the open white bundle uncertainly, as if it were a mysterious present, something she will not really want, which might require lying, false gratitude.

The scanty congregation shuffles out. Kate cannot quite bring herself to lay a guiding hand on the camel sleeve. It is as if her grandmother is trapped in an unbreakable bubble, small and far away. It's as if Kate is seeing her in a crystal ball.

'Kate! Your parents told me you'd be here.' Richard is waiting outside the church, muffled up in a scarf. 'Sorry I didn't ring. There's been a lot of family stuff.' Kate clings on to his arm joyfully. She can't kiss him because Granny is standing doubtfully by them. 'Can't you shake the old dear off?' he whispers. 'Well, I'll go on ahead then,' says Granny, suddenly astute. 'Are you sure you can get back alright?' Kate has a twinge of guilt, but Granny has already pottered off, moving slowly but determinedly down the long dark road. The two young people dawdle after the retreating figure. When she is out of sight they stop and kiss. Kate grips him as if she is falling, drowning. She wants to stay like this forever.

Walking

·

SALLY CAMERON

Walking is good for you. If you ask me, the world would be a much better place if everyone walked everywhere. There would be no wars for a start. If all the politicians and kings and queens and presidents had to travel by foot, they would be far too tired to start arguing with each other.

It's a long walk from my hospital ward to the nearest cafe. Seven miles, someone told me once. Fourteen there and back. They built the hospital just far enough from London to keep all the loonies out of sight. It's an imposing Victorian building, standing dark and austere in lush grounds big enough to be, for many, an entire world. The enormous iron gates at the end of the long drive are always open now, but no one bothers, or dares, to pass beyond. Remember when they thought the world was flat: if you went to the edge you'd drop off? Fat Stella and one or two of the young men sit at the entrance all day long watching the cars. Fat Stella cries all the time, loud, snotty sobs. Few people pass the hospital on foot, and the ones who do quicken their pace at the gates and pull their coats tightly around them. You can hear their thoughts: 'There but for the grace of God . . .' They look at Fat Stella not with pity but with fear. The rest of the patients slump on the benches in the garden, lie stiffly on the grass, or shuffle round and round the little pathways that lead nowhere. But you never see anyone leave. Except me, that is.

Today I button up the balding beaver collar of my mauve coat and nod at the gardener as I walk briskly up the drive, through the gates and on to the main road into London. I walk like a young woman. Everyone says so. ('Look at Mary – eighty-five, you know, isn't she marvellous!') One of the doctors told me I was a walking miracle, but I informed him that it was nothing to do with thaumaturgy, it was merely a matter of practice. It's a cold November day and beginning to spit with rain, but only my hands register the temperature. I watch them as they begin to turn blue, and then white.

'Put your gloves on, Mary,' George the nurse tells me as I am leaving, although he knows I will return with my gloves still in the pockets of my coat. Tonight he will reach for my numb hands, playfully admonishing me in his Irish lilt as he rubs them between his own.

The rush-hour traffic is slow and I cross the dual carriageway, weaving between the bonnets of crawling motor cars. With a raised hand I indicate for a large Ford to stop and the driver, in irritation, presses his horn and mouths angrily at me. I stop directly in front of his bonnet and fix him with a severe stare. My eyes have always been my best feature, so I'm told. ('Look at Mary's eyes – have you ever seen eyes so blue?'; 'Jesus, Mary, don't look at me like that – you give me the creeps!') The driver tries some ineffective gesticulations and then winds down his window.

'For Christ's sake, get a move on will you!'

I do not move.

'You stupid old cow – why can't you use the crossing like everyone else?'

Slowly, I raise my arm higher and point my index finger directly between his eyes. It never fails. Just a glimmer, the merest gulp in his neck, before he winds up the window and begins repeatedly pumping the horn, but it is enough. I raise my eyebrows and pass through the traffic to the big housing estate on the other side of the road. Down the hill, past the station, a school playground full of brown children, and a church with a sign saying 'Repent Now'. There are few people walking today. An angry mother pushing a pram and dragging a toddler by the arm. Two boys in school uniform running through the rain, laughing. As I reach the parade of shops I slow, pausing to look in the windows, but not for long. I am hungry.

One does not enjoy hospital food. The tea comes out of a giant metal pot with a suspicious white scum on top which disappears before the half-wits notice, and all the food smells of fish. I suppose they think everyone is too mad to care. So I have my breakfast at The Star Kebab House where the owner, George, gives me tea in a cup and saucer and fetches me a bun or a jam tart from the baker's next door. Today he is standing, as usual, in the doorway of the dark little cafe and he waves and smiles, beckoning me in.

'Hello old Mary – how's my Mary?'

I object to his choice of adjective, but then George is Turkish and they do things differently. Sometimes he sits with me at the little Formica table by the door and tells me stories about Turkey, showing me photographs of his children. He has told me his name many times but I always call him George. I call all men George.

Wrapping my hands around the hot teacup I wait for George to fetch me my cake. He is frying chips for the schoolgirl with the very black hair and very white face. Her eyes are pencilled dark in an attempt at adult sensuality, but she looks just like a small kitten, arching against the counter as she waits for her greasy bag of comfort. I have never seen George make a kebab. Although there is a long menu of different foreign dishes I've only ever seen him serve chips. The chips spit and a radio crackles and the girl moves her shoulders to the faintly discernible beat.

'There you go, my darling, careful now, they're hot.'

The girl counts out her change and saunters out, picking at the chips and avoiding my gaze, as most young girls do. Who really wants to believe that one day they, too, will be old? George wipes his hands on his apron.

'Okay, old Mary, what's it to be? I get you something nice eh?' Quickly he slips out of the cafe and returns with a currant bun in a paper bag.

'Okay for you? You want butter?'

I tell him I would like a plate and a knife too.

These days the buns are different. Bread too. Everything is too light, insubstantial. They put too much air in everything these days. When I was young my mother baked every morning, bread rolls, pies, rock buns, heavy doughs that you could feel inside you. I used to sit at the kitchen table making little figures out of the pastry cuttings, and my mother would let me bake the small effigies and eat them one by one. Heads first. She always said I was a strange little girl. After my father was killed in France my mother became deeply religious and took me to church every evening to pray for the destruction of the Huns, whom she regarded as the devil's own army. When the air raids started she looked on with contempt as our neighbours scurried down their cellars like rabbits, while she, proud and defiant, climbed on to the roof of our house to shout the wrath of God at the Zeppelins overhead. One evening, as we returned from church through the rubble of a raid, we passed a large hole in the ground, a six-foot crater. At its edge I could see the legs of a man, sticking up as though he were diving into a pool. When I think of it now I swear his feet were kicking, but that could hardly have been possible. My mother raised her face to the heavens, called out to the Almighty, and then grabbed my hand and pulled me away, covering my eyes. But not before I had peered into the hole and seen the man with no head.

My mother always said I was never the same again. Today, if you look through my fat hospital file you will find numerous references to the incident. Doctors love cause and effect. Often a keen student nurse will ask me gently and earnestly about my experiences of the war. But what I never tell them is that I was not in the least surprised by that body. I thought about it often, certainly, and my pastry people never had heads after that. I used to cut jagged necks with a knife and paint the edges with cochineal. But really, when I looked down into that hole, it was as if I had always known it would be there. If it had not been there it would have been somewhere else. For everyone, everywhere, there is a headless corpse just waiting around the corner. But I suppose most people never see it. Most people spend their lives looking the other way.

I finish my tea and take my cup to the sink behind the counter where George lets me wash up. I rinse it, as usual, twenty times, filling it to the brim, pouring the water down the sink, until George takes it from me. 'You English! Wasting water all the time. Give it here old Mary!' I always wash my cup. It seems only right as I have no money to pay for the tea. As I dry my hands a man comes into the cafe and seats himself at my table.

'Sausage, egg, chips – thanks,' he calls before burying his head in a newspaper.

I return to my seat, knocking the man's foot just slightly as I pull out my chair, and I see him glance from the side of his paper at my legs. He registers interest. I have good legs. Walking is good for the legs, and the young nurses say they would sell their souls for a pair like mine. In an instant the man's watery blue eyes have perused my entire body and come to rest, momentarily in horror, on my eighty-five-year-old face, before returning to the more succulent delights of the *Sun*. I ask him sweetly for a cigarette and, irritated, he reaches into his pocket without meeting my eyes. After such a blunder his guilty embarrassment makes him an easy touch and, were I in the habit of asking for money, I would be sure to make a small killing. I thank him for the cigarette and he passes me a box of matches, not bothering to tell me that his name isn't George. He has told himself that he would not touch me, not in a million years. But, as our eyes meet, we both know he would, if there was no one else. No one else to choose from and no one else to see him do it. They do it to old ladies like me. To children too and even, sometimes, to sheep.

George was my first. My mother was pleased that I had a sweetheart, for she thought I was spending far too much time in my bedroom cutting pictures for my scrapbook. I collected pictures of people out of old books, any people I could find. Ladies in beautiful ballgowns, beggars, priests, judges and tiny children in ruffles and lace. Of course I cut all their heads off before I pasted them into my book, and I joined their hands together to make a long, dancing line. My mother called it morbid, and so she was delighted when George, the grocer's son, began calling in the summer evenings to take me walking. Walking, however, was not all George had in mind.

It was only curiosity, but my mother was fond of telling me what that did to the cat. After George there were many others, for it was so easy to skip choir practice and walk on my own to the park, swinging my long plaits. There, behind the bushes, on the warm evenings of war, I learned how life was made. It seemed such a simple act, so simple that I was sure at first that there must be more. If death could be so varied, so enormously and expensively planned, then I was convinced that there must be more to the secret of creation than such a clumsy little manoeuvre. So I tried them all, city gents, soldiers, rich and poor, old and young, until I realised, watching each final grunt at my breast, that they all did exactly the same. As I said, it was only curiosity, but my mother had another word for it, and so did the doctors to whom she finally took me.

After they took the baby away I was locked in a bare white room. There were no windows and so I had to draw my headless companions on the white walls. I painted them in the cold, gelatinous gravy of my dinners, more success-fully in the thicker textures of my slop bucket, and finally, when I learned to bite the ends off my fingers, in blood.

My mother did not visit me. My only visitors were the nurses with the enormous, evil-smelling syringe. There was one nurse to hold my arms, one to hold my legs, and one to jab the needle into my arse. I was held in cold baths, wrapped in freezing, wet towels, strapped to a metal bed and fed through a rubber tube. When my mother wrote she talked of my freedom, like a carrot, but as the days turned into weeks and months I felt myself more free than ever before. There is a peculiar kind of freedom in a cell. The freedom to kick and shit and spit. The freedom to scream.

And, do you know, you can walk just as far in a cell as anywhere in the world. Three and a half paces, turn, three and a half paces back. It adds up. They thought it was the injections that made me quiet and, years later, the electric shocks. But I know I have always walked myself into silence. When I stopped talking altogether they gave me more shocks to bring back the words that I'd trampled underfoot, and finally they drilled a hole in my head, thinking they could find my voice there. Then they let me out of the cell and I began to walk up and down the long white corridor, through days and nights, days and years. I never saw my mother again. She sent me cards with pictures of Jesus and his disciples, and wrote to me of the cancer that was eating her bones.

'You did this to me, Mary,' she wrote when she was dying. 'You did this – you and the Huns.'

It's just stopped raining when I leave the cafe, waving goodbye to George.

'Take care now, Mary,' he tells me. 'Be good, Mary.'

That's what they all tell me. 'Be good.'

And mostly, these days, I am. Mostly now I am a sweet old lady in a fur-trimmed coat, a familiar figure on this route through the northern outskirts of London. A most suitable candidate, you might say, for community care. That's what they call it, the hospital closing down. They come in hordes now, these new ones, shivering down the long corridor which they call an architectural marvel. They visit us in the wards, and talk of preparation and of freedom, wearing their uniforms of blue jeans and earrings – the men too. They like to tell me that they understand. The painting woman wears lots of silk scarves and her blackened eyes are smug with secrets. We sit around a table with poster paint and sheets of sugar paper and she looks at my little headless figures wlth a grave pleasure. Fat Stella sometimes comes and paints too, but she never finishes her picture once she starts crying. The painting woman seems to like this; she holds Stella's hand and tells her she's doing well. When Stella's sobs begin the painting woman looks at her with pride, like she's hit the jackpot.

And then George comes to teach me how to cook. George, with his ponytail and his girl's voice who is young enough to be my grandson, comes to teach me how to live outside, in the pristine flats which they tell us will be our new homes. I like going to the supermarket. George lets me choose our lunch, and he enjoys explaining to me the value of our coins and notes. The ladies on the till call me 'love' and 'dear' and they nod and smile at George, telling him what a marvellous job he's doing. Usually I compliment George on the way back to the hospital, knowing that a bit of flattery will mean that he lets me sit with a cup of tea while he makes the lunch. It was George who took me to see the little box where they think I will live. I told him straight away that I would not go, that the hospital had suited me well enough for seventy years, but George patted my hand and told me that even the most wonderful opportunities take some getting used to. He told me I would do well on the outside, that my community orientation was already perfect and my social skills almost impeccable. He said they would all be proud of me.

As I step into the wet street outside the cafe I see the brick. It's lying beneath the scaffolding surrounding the newsagents. Really it is only half a brick, but it will do. No one bothers about the old lady stooping under the scaffolding to pick it up and so I have time to perfect my position in front of The Star Kebab House and take aim. My arms are nearly as strong as my legs. There is an explosion of shattering glass and suddenly everyone around me notices that I exist. George is running to his broken window, waving his arms. George is staring at the glass in his dinner, blood trickling from a splinter in his cheek. Georges everywhere stop and look at me as I wait for the sirens.

The two policemen are surprised to see their culprit. I tell them my full name and give the address of the hospital, which makes them nod at each other. One of them starts talking into his radio while the other ushers me firmly into the car.

'Shouldn't let them out really,' he murmurs to his partner. He grins at me, a boy's, nervous grin. 'Right then, love, let's get you back.'

I give him my sweetest smile and he looks relieved. Sometimes I enjoy a ride in a police car, and it looks impressive in my hospital file. Tonight George will sigh as he fills in the special report form. 'You've blown it again, Mary,' he will tell me, shaking his head. 'Now you're never going to get out of here.'

I'm rather looking forward to a month or two back on the locked ward. At this time of year it's always so dark and wet outside, and the locked ward has a nice stretch of blue carpet, thirty feet by ten, well-worn. As I said, walking is good for you. It doesn't matter where you go.

Mama B's Kitchen

•

JACQUELYN COLEMAN

It was called Mama B's kitchen on account of the fact that Mama B was forever cooking. Smells lived in the very timber of her old shack. Mama B lived in the back of the building, in a small room heated with kerosene and lit by candle. Her room was separated from the kitchen by a tattered and tired curtain of old red beads, which provided a small, make-shift screen. The kitchen was where Mama B made her living, did her laughing, talking, living and mending.

It was here where Mama B sold the patties, cookies, jerk pork, dumplings and salsify chicken that she made. The spice and seasoning sat on the wind and sailed as far out as Kennooga, the next town. Mama B's culinary skills were legendary. Her family had lived in the neighbourhood for years: her father, his father before him and his father before him. Mama B was known and she knew.

She knew every skeleton that creaked in the old town and the strings that held and strained each heart.

Mama B lived alone. Her flame, Joe, had long since passed on, caught a fever that made him thin and then turned him yellow. None of Mama B's witching skills could save him. She applied poultice, rhyme, she bled him, sweated him, she made God a thousand promises of all the things she would do right, change, quit doing, quit saying, quit thinking, but either God didn't hear or didn't believe her, for poor Joe went all the same.

Mama B was also a dangerous woman with a fearsome caste in her eye, and so much gold amongst her teeth that when she laughed her whole mouth caught as though aflame.

People called me Cochineal because that was my name. I was the colour of dark brown rum spat through with blood. The sun couldn't have burned or stroked me more. When Mama B called me Cochineal she dragged on the ending of my name, tugging and pulling at me. I never answered her until she called at least three, maybe four times, just to remind her that I couldn't be predicted, overlooked, or made small by her bigness. Everything came easily to her. She talked easily, walked easily, slept easily and laughed easily. No fear ever caught or halted her voice, step or glance. She trod as though she knew every step before it was taken.

The only thing I had ever been easy about and sure of was the rose of my life, who hung like a bright constant light, exposing every crevice and corner. And so he had licked my skin through and through, my lover, Ben. We had rubbed noses, linked toes and made real our fantasies till there were none left and we settled snugly into what we knew, retracing and feeling old familiar and centred pathways. When we kissed, he still sucked my mouth as though he drank from a custard apple, leaving my lips large and full, pouting although they didn't contrive to.

Ben had taken me to Dawson city. We were the only Black people there, but no one much bothered, they were all too taken with gold fever to mind us. I nearly lost my toes the cold bit so hard, and Ben never found any gold, at least not enough. The buyers got rich, the hunters got stolen from and disillusioned. I sung and earned a little money, thrown at my feet as I stood on the redwood piano of the Criddle Creak Saloon. My voice always rattled my chest, as it sprang from me, like an elastic band, hitting walls, touching hearts and smarting me on the high notes till my eyes watered.

I could sing. I could always sing. Even now I was still asked to sing at christenings, weddings and funerals. I liked christenings the best. They were always full of hope and welcoming. I learned to breathe properly, I stood with my arms folded lightly just below my breasts and sang from a special place called my diaphragm. With my voice I imagined touching the moon and making my God smile. I sang for my lover, Ben. I eventually sang our food and fare home from Dawson city. I sung the bright gold in his teeth and the new roof on our house.

With all that Eskimo kissing and loving came babies, tumbling from my body one after the other. We had seven in all, two we lost, but we had and kept five. I was a lover, a singer, a mother, and that was enough.

Mama B had always liked my man. I knew. Her voice

was manicured when she spoke to him, filed down to a fine syrup to call on his masculinity. The gentler she spoke, the gruffer his reply sounded, for she embarrassed him with all her seeming nakedness.

Willy Boy, Ray and Donnie, our three sons, worked with Ben, and Desree and Nes, our teenage daughters, just sat around looking wide-eyed and beautiful. They were the twins. A little slow. A little too much or too little of something had caused it. I'd fallen; something; no one was quite sure what had caused the girls to be simple. They were like big, beautiful brown dolls, wide-eyed and frightening. They were quiet girls, they looked inside themselves. They liked pockets, buttons, zips, petticoats, drawers and envelopes. They liked to prise their brown fingers inside or underside to get into the little spaces and hide there where it was dark and safe. They hummed and rocked, sitting on the porch shelling endless peas and smiling, and often, with no warning, they would wander. At times they'd get lost and Willy Boy, my eldest, would usually find them down by the river, bathing their feet and braiding their hair. My two beautiful dolls with no lights behind their eyes. Their father stepped around them delicately, carefully, as though a touch of breath might break them. When they were younger and out of step with the other children, I knew it hurt him to regard them and he kept them to the periphery of his vision and to the periphery of his life.

Mama B walked toward me in all her finery, her hat perched firmly on her head, her smile fixed to her face. She stopped and stood by me whilst I filled pails of water.

'Cochineal, I'm heading over to Kentown.'

'H'mm, h'mm,' I nodded.

'Visiting my sister, Yeppy. You remember Yeppy?' she said, straightening her frock. I nodded.

'How's her bad leg? Didn't she take a fall last summer?'

'Yes, and the rheumatism's been biting ever since.' She turned her head and spat to the side of the road.

'I've made her a poultice, and I have a fine brew of tea to set her right,' she added.

Mama B stood for a long time, shuffling and waiting to say what she really wanted to. She followed me back to my house.

'Something else, Mama B?' I asked.

'Yes, Cochineal. Something else.' She gripped her hand-bag tightly before her.

'It's about your Willy Boy.'

I was puzzled, curious, my heart raced a little and I waited. She lowered her voice. 'I can't be sure, but my mind tells me it's him. For the past few weeks when I'm in my back room at night, and my lights are down low, I've seen someone snooping, lurking out there in the back, watching me through the back window. The other night I called out and I saw a figure, he ran out back and I swear it was your Willy Boy, watching me.'

I looked at her in disbelief, trying to make some sense of her cloud of words. Her eyes never left mine and she said, 'It was him, Cochineal.'

This woman, whose body laughed at age was the object of my son's green sex peeking at her, wondering, lusting, why else would he watch her?

'Why? Why would he watch you?' I asked.

She turned away to the side. 'He's a young man. They have ideas.'

But she was old, she was not young.

'If it was late and dark you couldn't be sure it was Willy Boy. It could have been someone else, someone looking for food, anything.'

'It was Willy Boy, watching me. I was undressing, fixing my hair. It was him.'

I looked down. The woman was a reptile, her brazen womanness was like a long wicked leg wrapped around a tree, blending with the bark and the branch.

'I'll talk to him. I'll see that it won't happen again.'

She shook out the bell of her frock and the sweet smell of talc swept up and disguised her. I watched her as she headed for the bus station.

Later that day, we all sat down and ate chicken soup, peaches and jello. I let everyone filter off to bed and asked Willy Boy to help me clear up. I watched his face, looking for a sign, a motion. He was, as always, orderly and careful. He tidied, and sorted. He hummed a little.

'Willy Boy.'

He stopped and turned to me. He knew the tone, soft but sober, gone was the light and easy-over supper chatter.

'Yeah, Mama?'

'Have you been watching what you shouldn't be?'

He cocked his head over to one side, I faced him squarely. 'Looking, snooping. Watching a woman at night through her window.'

He hung his head, his arms limp by his side. There were no sides for him to reach out to. He had not known what I would find or ask. I was his mother discovering a secret, a known water-washed stone, smooth and cool on one side with a rough, rude underbelly on the other. He was ashamed, and would have preferred to die than to face me with this, his sorry and fearful sexuality. Finally, he nodded.

'Okay . . . now all I want you to do is to stop it. No more. Okay . . . and it'll be forgotten,' I said. He nodded. Two hot tears ran slowly down his face. I misread his tears for shame, for they were the first signs of a brooding and growing anger. He left the kitchen, and that night I washed again every clean and dry plate and dish in the pantry.

The summer turned to fall, changing colours, scents and mood. Out came all the warmer clothes, and Mama B and I washed our laundry together by the river. There was no more snooping and Willy Boy worked long and hard hours, although he was more quiet than usual. The early autumn fair came, and with it a cosmic collection of fire-eaters, dancers, magicians and tired, sad old bears. Fortunes were told, paradise plums sold, and children's high-pitched squeals filled the afternoons and early evenings for a good week. Jake Madrigal was the proprietor, a giant of a man with eyes that sat deep and too-close together. My girls thought he was God, owing to his top hat, height and curious ability to yodel. He had supper with us and swapped fireside stories with my husband.

By the first frost of winter, Desree had taken to her bed. She shuddered under the blankets and her sister Nes still smiled. Their father thought Desree had gone mad, a little further down the path; he would never catch her. She wouldn't let me come near her. She just slept and ate. She would howl if I came near her. Her hair grew dirty and matted, and her room came to smell hot and stuffy but she liked it so and closed all the windows, putting crumpled paper at the foot of the door, filling the space between floor and door. I sent Donnie for Dr Reed. Dr Reed was a short, thick-set man of very few words. When the Doctor entered her room, Desree began to make a loud whooping noise. Dr Reed shook his head.

'Hysteria,' he mumbled.

Oh, that it had been hysteria. Nes roamed throughout the house, thumb in mouth, walking from room to room, lost and looking for her sister who by apparent madness had deserted her.

Dr Reed prescribed Sercea herb tea and frequent poultices made of wild-cat tongue. Desree grew fuller, fatter although she ate very little.

Mama B maintained a small distance from my family; Willy Boy had set her uneasily at odds with the woman she felt herself to be. I walked wearily to the kitchen, she was busy baking sweetmeats, her hair tied back from her face and her hands working rhythmically kneading and loving the dough. With every round pat she made, she popped a raisin into her mouth and added several to each cake, adding dried cherries and cinnamon.

'My, you are fretting, Cochineal. What did the Doctor say?' Mama B stopped and looked at me.

'Hysteria. Influenza. Fever. A chill . . . He said she was young and that it would soon pass. I don't know, B, something ain't right but the chile won't let me near her.'

Mama B promptly dried her hands upon her apron, and

just as she was, bade me follow her as she walked to my home. She opened the door to the front porch and climbed up the old, rickety steps. We followed her, myself and all the others in the household, in a silent, orderly procession. Mama B entered the room, tall like a willow tree, waving her arms and cooing softly with her eyes closed. She stepped cautiously and slowly towards the bed, Desree lay sleeping and Mama B gently placed her cool palm on Desree's forehead.

'Shh,' Mama B whispered.

The room was silent though we all stood around the bed watching and waiting. Desree stirred but her eyes remained closed. Her fists remained clenched and Mama B gently uncurled one fist to remove a tiny gold pin. A fancy tie-pin. I took it from her and stared at it, wondering and fearing. Mama B's hands travelled over Desree's body, searching, feeling and sensing. Finally Mama B nodded, drew back the sheets, stood and breathed heavily.

Mama B looked at me, her expression both sad and serious. I feared what was coming. She took my damp hand and led me slowly from the room. We walked into the parlour and she closed the door quietly behind us. Holding my hands, we sat facing each other, and Mama B's eyes held mine.

'Cochineal, I don't know how to say this . . . there is no easy way, and that fool Dr Reed should have known,' she wrung her hands. 'Desree's with child.'

My beautiful brown china doll suddenly fell and broke into a thousand small pieces. I gripped the tie-pin harder, tighter and slowly drew on its meaning.

'She's just a child,' I said. My voice had shrunk to the back of my throat.

Mama B looked away. 'I know,' she said.

Just then the door flew open. It was Ben, his eyes were half-wide with madness and fury.

'I know,' he hissed. 'I know.'

The three of us used up that small parlour place, pacing, sighing, crying and cursing.

'But who is the father?' asked Mama B.

I held out the gold tie-pin which showed the initials J.M.

Ben seized the pin and after scrutinising it dashed it to the floor.

'Jake Madrigal,' I said numbly.

Mama B nodded. We sat for a while, which grew into forever, each on the edge of our own wooden, hard-backed chair. Eventually Ben spoke. 'Mama B. She can't have this child. It can't be. Mustn't be.'

Mama B was silent.

'She's a child . . .' he said and for the first time I saw my Ben weep.

Mama B slowly stood, and said she would call in later. Her voice was barely audible as she left the room.

'Mama B must help,' Ben insisted. 'She must.'

I followed Mama B back to her shack. We walked in silence until we reached the door to her kitchen.

'No, Cochineal. I will not wash my hands with blood. Not blood. Not this,' she shook her head.

Desree's stomach grew round and large and she hugged her dolls and teddy bears closer to her. Nes followed her sister devotedly carrying shelled peas in the lap of her frock.

'Ain't right. That old witch knows how to put it right but she won't. Ain't right. No way,' Willy Boy paced the floor.

'Donnie and the boys will find that Jake Madrigal and put the whole thing to rights,' he nodded.

My brow grew heavy and tight, and I aged, from autumn to winter all in a matter of weeks, all joy and hope had left me.

'But that friggin' bitch up yonder, she can fix Desree, make it right.' Willy Boy worked up a hate, an ice-hot hate for Mama B. His hate grew on shame and fed on a deepening shame and resentment. But Mama B wasn't for turning. Not babies, not children, not life. She had always wanted children. Young'uns. They never came, and she wouldn't take life from a body. Children were for breathing, living and growing. She called it the Devil's work.

She wouldn't turn. Ben visited, Ray and Donnie visited, all begging. But Mama B wouldn't turn. The village knew of Desree's child and all looked to Mama B for Desree's deliverance, but none came. People stopped buying food from Mama B's kitchen. She held back, so they held back, and Mama B receded into the small space of her back room.

Early in the spring, in the small hours of the night, Nes woke me from my bed. She dragged me over to the window and pointed. At first sleep clouded my eyes, but as they slowly focused I came to see more clearly a fire, roaring and raging, gorging itself full of building. It was Mama B's kitchen.

I ran from the house, Nes skipping behind me. I ran screaming Mama B's name, but the kitchen was fully ablaze and I, with others, struggled helplessly to put out the fire. Ray, Donnie and Willy Boy cast long shadows and stood silently watching. All around them people panicked, dashed, shouted, struggled, but my three sons stood still, watching.

The heat scorched my hair but I continued throwing futile buckets of water until the last flame belched and withered. Mama B's rings and belongings were found amongst the ashes. She had died alone in the flames. Old Sam Carver had seen her tumble and fall.

My sons had stood watching until the last flame had died.

Willy Boy spat, turned and said, 'Best place for the old witch.'

I knew then of the work his hands had performed. They had killed her, killed her for not turning, killed her for not being who and what they wanted her to be, killed her for being Mama B.

Her remains were buried on Lockhart Hill and my Ben made a small wooden cross and carved her name on the face of a large boulder which became her headstone. Desree placed yellow daffodils at the head of the grave each spring, whilst her daughter, Mary, sat nearby, breathing and playing in the sun.

Famous Last Words

.

SALLY REEVES

I spent the six weeks of the summer holidays when I was twelve waiting for my father to die. I sat for hours every day in the large alcove at the top of the stairs where our childhood books and toys were stored, waiting for grand-children.

There was a window above the alcove and, when we were younger, my friend Tessa and I would stretch rugs from the banister to the window-sill, securing them with books, for privacy. We hadn't done many things which needed privacy, apart from poring over the medical dictionary which had cut-away diagrams of the male and female sex organs. But it had felt secure, stuffy and dusty under the old plaid rugs which had been used for picnics or to tuck us up on the set-tee by the fire when we had been ill. I felt like putting the rugs up again, but it was the hottest summer I'd ever known.

All the windows in the house were open except in Dad's room because he seemed to feel cold all the time.

I still spent time in the alcove, reading. There was a miniature, child-size armchair patterned with faded roses in there and I could still squeeze into it and stretch my legs out on top of the toy chest. I didn't read much that summer though, mostly I just waited.

My mother sat in the spare bedroom with him, knitting. He'd been moved in there because they had been disturbing each other in the double bed. Now she had moved a camp bed in there too, and slept with him at night.

We'd been doing *A Tale of Two Cities* that year at school, so the significance of her knitting didn't pass me by. I could hear the needles sometimes, tic, tic, tic, and the occasional rustle of the pattern. I wondered if it disturbed him, as he drifted in and out of sleep. He'd always liked Dickens, too.

I leaned on the open door and kicked at the door frame.

'Ssh, dear,' she said, not looking up.

'What are you knitting now?' I asked in a stage whisper.

She looked at me in a puzzled way, as though I'd asked rather an odd question, then held up a shapeless red mass.

'It was a jumper but I'm not sure now, it's outgrown itself. I may have to unpick it.'

My mother was super-precision knitter number one. Perfect dolls' clothes, gloves, socks, jumpers and cardigans had leapt off her needles for as long as I could remember. Strange, the things that make you realise something's really wrong.

My eldest sister was downstairs, cooking for hours on end. She made thin, nourishing soups for Dad, casseroles and pies for us, and then recipes from her school cookery book which she'd found in the cupboard in her old bedroom. She made one each day, in the order she'd learned them: shortbread, fairy cakes, rock cakes, swiss roll, Victoria sponge, apple pie, sausage rolls, vol au vents; girls' boarding-school recipes. She had left school five years before.

I'd wander down there and she'd have everything spread out on the kitchen table. Ingredients in bowls in a row, waiting patiently for their turn like pensioners in the post-office queue. She had her old, blue school exercise-book propped up in front of her, ink splotched and with dried flour-mixture finger marks on its pages.

'Four ounces of raisins,' she'd say out loud. 'Stir into the mixture.'

I'd lick the bowls and eat the cakes as soon as possible after they came out of the oven, taking them off the cooling tray and burning my mouth. I ate more of them than anyone. Our mother would have the odd bite with a cup of tea and then leave the rest to go soggy in the saucer.

My middle sister would dash in and cram something into her mouth on the run. The cooking sister would put a small, perfect round of sugared shortbread, or a fairy cake with little wings poised ready to flutter away, on a plate on my father's bedside table.

If he woke up and she was there, she'd say, 'Just try a little of this, Daddy. Remember how you liked my cooking from school. You'd come in on a Tuesday and say "Cooking day, what's for tea?"'

Sometimes he'd smile vaguely up at her, but the food

was never touched. They were often still there the following day when the new offering arrived. She would take it downstairs and throw it in the bin. If I was the one who removed them, I'd eat them, secretly, feeling guilty, as though I was eating something of his.

In the evenings she phoned her husband Derek, up north, and told him what was happening. She would cup both her hands round the receiver and lean over, so her hair fell round it.

'Worse, I think,' she said. 'No, not really. Just cooking mostly. No, I haven't yet, I'll tell them soon, it never seems to be the right moment. No, maybe you're right. I will.' Then she whispered, 'I love you. I miss you too,' before she put the receiver down and stood there for a little while before she went back into the kitchen.

My middle sister was frenetic at that time, she was always doing something, in and out, up and down stairs, she couldn't sit still. She saw friends, she played tennis, she swam and she rode her bicycle to the village on endless errands to buy packets of dried fruit or flour, a tin of soup, a bar of chocolate, any excuse.

'Get me a Mars Bar,' I shouted, 'and a Kit Kat.'

I'd eat them one after the other and then ask her to get me more on her next trip. No one ever said anything. Mother just left money on the dresser and we helped ourselves. My shorts felt tight and I had to leave the top buttons undone.

I wasn't sure what I was waiting for, I just wanted to be around. I'd worked out that he was dying, although I didn't believe it all the time. No one had told me, but I'd learned to eavesdrop to find out information. I was a quiet child and people forgot I was there. I knew which floorboards and stairs creaked in the house.

'It's "C", I'm afraid,' my mother had whispered to my aunt several weeks before. 'No, not good.' Then, another time, 'Weeks they say. No, I haven't told them, it's best they don't know.'

Then, at times, to other enquirers and to us, she said, 'Of course he'll get better. It's just a matter of time. He needs a lot of rest to build up his strength again.'

We all knew, of course, but no one said the 'D' word either.

I think I was waiting for him to say something but I wasn't sure what. Some famous last words, just for my ears. I knew about death-bed speeches. 'It is a far, far better thing that I do' and all that. It was also something we said at school. Someone would say 'I think he really likes me' or 'I think I did well in the test' and someone else would say, slightly mockingly, 'Huh, famous last words'.

He was awake sometimes and he would even sit up and drink, but he was so thin and yellow. He held out his hand to me and I was scared it would fall apart like newspaper that had been too close to the fire. His hands were cold and bony and he looked flat under the eiderdown, as if he was hardly there.

'Hello, Susy,' he said. 'How are you today?'

'I'm fine, Dad. How are you?'

'Much the same. Shall we have a game of draughts?'

We had always played games, we didn't even have a television then. I used to have to go to my friends' houses to watch *Bonanza* and *Z Cars*.

Sometimes he was asleep before I'd even got the board out. Sometimes he made a few moves and occasionally we would even finish a game. I tried to let him win, like he used to with me when I was younger so I didn't get discouraged.

'Now, now,' he said, 'you must try harder.'

He was a schoolteacher. He used to say that when he read our reports.

Our end of the village was quiet but, sitting there on the landing, I could hear layers of sound unfolding, the harder I listened, the more I heard. Nearby, the knitting needles clicking, downstairs the bump of bowl and stir of wooden spoon; just outside, bees buzzing, birds singing; further away a dog barking as though it was shut in and lonely, the bark occasionally rising to a *Hound of the Baskervilles* howl; the hum of cars on the main road; a voice calling out to someone; children laughing and shrieking on the village recreation ground.

The nurse visited every day and the doctor every other. They tapped on the front door and opened it without waiting, coming slowly up the stairs carrying leather bags. They didn't notice me. My mother had told other people not to call, she said he didn't want visitors. Some of my friends came round to start with but I would never go out, so they stopped coming. Tessa was in Devon, riding horses and bossing her little brothers. Her parents had asked me to go too but I'd refused.

One day my middle sister brought a young man home with her. She left him standing down in the hall and went up to our father's room. I watched him over the banisters, he was looking around, fiddling with his hands. He was short and stocky, he looked awkward and hot. He wore large square glasses with heavy dark frames, and he kept pushing them up when they slid down his nose.

She said something to my mother. I heard their voices, then I ducked while she went back downstairs.

'He's asleep,' she said, sounding disappointed.

'Never mind, Judy, I'll meet him some other time.'

'I'm not sure how much other time we've got,' she said, and he put his arms round her and cuddled her. Then they went out again. I'd never seen him before.

She brought him back the next day and the one after that, and the same thing happened each time. Dad wasn't awake much any longer. I went and sat on his bed sometimes when Mum was out of the room, going to the toilet or finding more wool. She had abandoned the red mess and started on blanket squares.

'Don't disturb him,' she said when she came back in. 'He's resting.'

Once I got under the bed and lay there among the dust balls, crumpled tissues and his abandoned slippers. He never moved for the hour and a half I was there.

The second day I went downstairs and said hello to Judy's boyfriend.

'I'm Roy,' he said. 'And you must be Susy. Hello.'

He seemed nervous and the hand he held out was stodgy and damp. His forehead was shiny and sweaty.

'Rather a weak handshake, I'm afraid,' I imagined Dad saying. 'What does he do for a living?'

My mother had come down to meet him and we all stood there for a while, not quite knowing what to say. She wanted to be back upstairs, but she thought it was rude to go too quickly.

'Why don't you make – er a cup of tea, Judy?' she said.

'Roy,' she said. 'It's Roy, Mother.'

She started back up the stairs and then turned round.

'I'm sure Judy's father will be pleased to meet you soon. He just needs a lot of rest at the moment.'

She carried on up the stairs. Judy sighed and looked at him, then they went into the kitchen. I followed Mother upstairs to my alcove.

Evenings were dreadful. We sat around in Dad's room to eat whatever Pat had cooked for us. Usually he was asleep, so we'd whisper when we had anything to say. Mostly we didn't, so there were long silences, with cutlery ringing harshly on china and the sound of our swallowing loud in the hot room.

I would go and lie on my bed after we'd washed up. Then I'd allow myself to read to escape and get tired so I could sleep. I went back to my Enid Blyton books, going off to Kirren Island with the Famous Five. I put myself into bed when I felt tired, not bothering to clean my teeth but always saying goodnight to Dad, whether he was awake or asleep.

One day, at the end of August, he was sitting up when I went in to see him in the morning. Mum was sitting beside him on the bed, smiling.

'Your father feels better today,' she said.

'That's good. Can I get you anything, Dad?'

'We might have a game of chess later, Susy. Maybe a cup of tea for your mother and I.'

I went downstairs but Pat was already bustling about, laying a tray with an embroidered cloth she had made at school. There were two slices of sponge cake on a doily on one of the best plates.

'I'll take it up,' she said. 'Give me a few minutes and then you come up.'

I ate a quarter of the cake and then went up. They were all smiling at each other and Mum had been crying and was mopping her eyes with a handkerchief.

'You're going to be an auntie, Susy,' Pat said.

'When?'

'February.'

I didn't know what to say. I've never been a great babies person, but my mother was filling in for me.

'Isn't it wonderful? I've been longing to be a granny. I can start knitting for it. What colour do you think, Pat?'

I looked at my dad and he had a glazed, distant look in his eyes, although he was holding Pat's hand and smiling.

About an hour later, Judy came in with Roy, introduced him to Dad and announced that they were getting engaged. They had known each other about a month. Slightly less tears of joy and another out-of-it look from Dad, but they did their best. We toasted the news with sparkling wine. Roy worked in a bank apparently.

Later, everyone drifted off. Mum allowed herself a rare trip to the village shop to buy some white wool and baby knitting patterns. Pat went to cook another cake and Judy and Roy went to look at jewellery shops.

Dad and I had our game of chess. What else did I have to offer? He already knew I'd come top in English, second to bottom in Chemistry and in the middle in everything else. That was all I had in the big news stakes. He was getting very tired, his eyes kept closing and his head jerking. He didn't seem to notice me making stupid moves so he could win quickly.

When I was putting the pieces in the box, he lay down and said, 'Well, Susy, births, marriages and deaths.' Then he fell asleep. He didn't speak again, as far as I know. He died two days later.

I'm sitting writing all this down thirty years later. It's amazing what you can remember when you put your mind to it. I wonder if my mother can hear the scratch of my pen and the rough, friction sound of my hand and jumper moving across the paper. Maybe it annoys her and she would prefer me to knit, but I never did learn. She's so confused, she couldn't tell me anyway. Maybe she doesn't even know I'm here. She often doesn't know my name.

Judy and Roy are on their way back from Australia. Their flight should be taking off about now, but it's unlikely they'll be here in time. Pat is up in Manchester, visiting another hospital, maternity instead of geriatric. Her long-awaited first grandchild was born yesterday after five miscarriages. She has to stagger her visiting so as not to meet Derek. They split up twenty years ago and still hate each other's guts. She'll be back down tomorrow, but there are no cooking facilities here.

And me, I'm good at waiting. No great expectations.

Scarlet Dancing

·

MAGGIE HARRIS

Millie was at the waterpump already. Bee, panting, placed her buckets down on the wet stone and fanned cool air across her face. 'And that's before I fill up mih buckets, child', she said by way of greeting.

'You want for take it easy', the other woman said. Taking her own advice she leaned back against the wall where her muddy toes splayed out between yellow flip-flops.

Bee breathed one slow breath at a time to counteract the long walk up the hill. The sun seemed hotter already; or maybe it was the day with its early starts that seemed longer.

Millie looked her full in the face. 'What happen girl, you ain't sleep good?'

'Sleep all right on its own,' Bee said slowly, 'left to its own. If a person was left to sleep their natural sleep it would conquer the ills of all mankind, I tell you.'

'I see.' Millie sniffed. 'Madam next door still performing then?'

'Still performing, child. A body could be turning in its natural rhythm then, lo and behold! the devil comes riding in on horseback!'

'Well, they do say his servants ride at dawn . . .'

'Millicent, you know I wouldn't sin my soul by casting aspirations.'

'Not at all, Sister Bee. Everybody know your mouth don't wash on anybody – at least not without just cause.'

'I just don't know how long I can put up with all this commotion.'

'What happening this morning then?'

'Same as usual, only worse. Before the cock himself was up, those jalousies were knocking back against that wall like it does every four-day-morning, whether it rain or shine. Lord only knows how the poor mother don't catch her death with that cold breeze whistling through those windows. She ain't well, you know. The other day I see her holding her belly and the doctor herself drive up last week.'

'And the girl still singing and dancing up the place?'

'Yes, my dear. Loud and clear her voice is ringing through the neighbourhood with all kinda rendition of song that come out of that radiogram. Even Sunday morning and all. Imagine!' Millie sucked her teeth.

'But what she want to get up so early and carry on so? She think is party time or she don't have respect for people sleep?' Bee shrugged tiredly as Millie went on. 'Why she want to carry on like it was day? I mean, this is a recent occurrence, eh Sister Bee?'

'Well you know that child has always been strange. She set out doing everything different to anybody else right from the day she learn to walk.'

'Yes, that was quick quick, if I remember rightly.'

'Nine months old, my girl. She just upped and waltzed off her mother lap one day. I was there, witness to all. Those were the days when her mother would have decent relations with her neighbours, you know? When The Man was still here, remember?' Millie crossed her arms across her breasts and sucked her teeth again loudly. 'Well, he was a lot o' use eh? Take his little bit o' sweetness and gone.'

Bee sniffed. 'Well, that ain't nothing new. He hang around a lot longer than a lot o' them do. Not to mention anybody name,' she added hastily, watching Millie's eyebrow starting to jump. 'But what I could never understand is why that woman keep that stupid name of his for Scarlet? I mean, who is doing all the work and raising of the child on her own? What she want to hold on to a damfool name like Danzzing for is totally beyond my escalations. But, going back to this business with Scarlet, you know that child really got it in for me ever since last New Year time when I catch her at her blasphemous behaviour. You remember the antics I catch her at in St Ignatius' ruin? I feel like my soulcase was going to drop down dead on the spot! There I was going about my business like any decent body, I think I was looking for some wild bora or something – and I walking past the church and I hearing music of all things coming out from there! So I put my head round the doorway – watching I don't mash up my foot on some rotten wood or rusty nail and catch tetnus and dead, you know – and who don't I see but Scarlet Danzzing on top o' that old altar piece! This child is doing some kinda jumping up and stamping up there in her mother old high heel shoe that she don't need anymore since The Man gone; the arms them and the legs is going to hell and fro in all kinda different direction in some wild man dance! I have, old as I am, never seen the like in a young girl yet, lessen is Carnival time down below and that ain't for the righteous as we know'.

Bee paused for breath, taking her old Panama off and fanning herself with it. 'And the cut eye!' she continued. 'The cut eye the child pass me when I grab her arm and drag her back home! I tell you, Millicent, if looks could kill I woulda be six foot under already.'

'And what she mother say again?'

'Say? Say? That mother of hers stand up straight and tell me how Scarlet does have her own ways of doing things! Hmph! I tell you, I just don't know what this world is coming to at all!' She bent to pick up the bucket. 'I gon see you, girl, I lef' some pepper-pot on a slow boil, it gon dry up. Morning then.'

'Morning Sister Bee, take it easy.'

The sun was taking its time coming up this morning. Droplets of water from last night's rain still hung onto the thick green leaves of the rubber tree. The wind had even blown down some green mangoes. Bee picked up a few and tucked them in her apron pocket.

Millicent walked up the path cursing. She slammed her buckets down and ran the tap water over her legs.

'What happen to your foot them this morning, girl?'

'Some jackass car come tearing past me down the road and splash right through the blasted puddle. I'm sure these people does do it deliberate to show off.'

'Is like they have to tell us they got car, like we ain't got eyes or something.'

'I didn't think you was coming for water this morning, Sister Bee. I thought your son finish knocking up that water butt he promise you?'

'That good-for-nothing! Is how much Sundays he coming to build it? Him with his sweet-talk only know to walk with flowers 'pon a Sunday.'

'He should feel shame. You not getting any younger, and since he get the little job he can get some material and thing, nuh?'

'Child, we can only raise our children, how they turn out is up to them. But he is the least of my troubles. Since that Scarlet mother dead and she gone off God knows where my body still can't get back to normal.'

'You still ain't sleeping good?'

'Up before God's sun. This last couple o' years I get so used to that Scarlet making all kinda noise is like my body adapt to she own rhythm! Sunday morning especial I lie there expecting she to break out with she ructiousness. You remember how I tell you she used to save up all the bad bad song just for Sunday? How she used to treat the world to song at the top of her voice and not with nothing appropriate neither like "Morning has Broken", but things like "Wings of a Dove" and that thing she call "I watch my man do the pepper-pot jive" which I never hear on no radio?'

Millicent nodded.

'Well is like the quiet is worse than the noise, you know?'

'Is only us old people left here now. All everybody is running look job, get apartment, get car and thing. Even the parson tell me how Sans Souci parish is taking up all his time, how he got to counsel this body and that body, somebody getting drunk and beating up somebody else and thing, and how he gon have to slim down his visits up here to once a month, and why us old people don't go live with our children?!'

'Eh eh! Is who he think he is?'

'We can't blaspheme, girl, we can't blaspheme.'

Millicent made her way across the mountain path. Ma Nellie gave her a wave as she rocked herself in the hammock under her house shelling peas. Millie declined her offer of some lime drink saying she was going across to visit Sister Bee. 'Well, you just see you call in on your way back,' the old woman grunted. Millie pushed open Bee's gate which swung back easily, with no sound of the creaks it usually made. Millie sniffed; like she can smell paint too.

She walked up the doorstep. 'Sister Bee! Sister Bee! You here?' She pushed open the door and walked through to the back verandah where Bee was sitting on her rocker. 'Sister Bee, I come to see if you all right. Since I come back from visiting my daughter in Sans Souci – two, three days now – I ain't see you fetching water. Is where you been?'

Bee patted the easy chair next to her for Millie to sit down. 'I am fine. I am just fine girl', she said, beaming. 'And I don't think you will be seeing me up there again.'

Millicent frowned, was the old lady in her dotage already? But she seemed all there . . .

From across the backyard Millie suddenly heard the sound of a radio turned on so loud she jumped. The words of the song were clear clear: 'I watch my man do the pepper-pot jive . . .' She turned to Bee, her mouth open.

Bee smiled and started to join in on the next line: '. . . and he move his tail like he on a beehive.' She laughed, '"Bee"hive! You get it Millie? Yes, Scarlet is back. And look!' She pointed down towards the yard. 'She make me a brand new waterbutt and all, so I won't be struggling up top any longer.' She leaned over the verandah. 'Scarlet! Scarlet child! Come over and have some coolade with me and my friend Millie!'

Rosie's Tongue

·

ALISON MACLEOD

My mother said she should have seen it coming.

At the age of five I could roll my tongue into a fat little sausage and swallow it whole. By the time I was ten I could out-twist any tongue-twister while chewing gum at the same time; she was selling sea shells down by the seashore faster than it was ever thought possible. And in the schoolyard, in the bite of mid-winter, my tongue would glide lickety-split off the frosted metal of the monkey bars while other kids were left dangling for dear life by the tips of their tongues.

It was when I turned thirteen that my mother said she would have to take me to see Dr Freeman. Things had got out of hand, she said: I couldn't hold my tongue.

Dr Freeman's office was in the new five-storey Shopping Village on the main road. While my mother window-shopped our way to the waiting room, I tried to make a mental plan of the nearest exits. There were none. Only potted plastic palm trees as far as the eye could see.

Dr Freeman's receptionist was wearing a badge on her peach lapel. It read, 'HI! I'M RAQUEL.'

'HI RAQUEL!' I reciprocated. 'I'M ROSIE!'

Raquel looked up from her appointment book, a little shaken. She had wings of yellow hair that defied gravity. The sight of them made me want to fly. She turned and addressed my mother. 'You can go right through. Dr Freeman's expecting you.'

With her stalwart handbag on one arm, my mother guided me up the narrow corridor with the other. The door was open – I could just see upholstered walls – then it slammed shut without warning.

'I do apologise,' said a well-modulated voice. 'It's the wind.'

I turned and found him seated behind a desk-top picture of himself, his wife, and two slavering labradors. 'You've got air-conditioning,' I pointed out. I had to keep my wits about me.

'Please, have a seat.'

Dr Freeman wore contact lenses that turned his eyes a technicolor green. He leaned forward, across his desk, and smiled comfortingly. He was trying to mesmerise me, and I knew it. So did my mother, but she only looked on, smiling her you-know-best, I-sacrifice-my-only-daughter-to-you smile.

'Rosie,' he began, 'I want you to tell me why you are here.' He hadn't blinked once since we had walked into the room. He wanted me to confess.

I swallowed. 'I–'

'Go on.'

'My mother–'

She stopped smiling. 'That's right. Blame it on me, Rosie. Tell the doctor it's all my . . .' Her words died away. She was wearing half a dozen stray rubber bands around one of her wrists – household finds that were always on the verge of coming in handy. Now she was anxiously twisting a thick red one, threatening her own blood supply.

I slapped her martyred wrist. 'Cut it out, Mom.' I returned to the doctor. 'My mother says I've up and gone crazy with hormones.' I gave him a flirtatious little wink.

His green eyes did not so much as flicker. But I heard them say, 'Tell me about your dreams, Rosie.'

I looked away. I wouldn't give in. I took a deep breath. 'Right. Pencil ready? By the time I'm sixteen, I want to be in the Ice Capades. I want to wear one of those little silver skirts, and when I spin, I'll wow everyone because I won't be wearing any underwear. By the time I'm twenty-one, I want to be a starlet, the old-fashioned kind. I want to be the heroine with the banana ringlets who wins the hearts of all by tying the hero with the square jaw to the railway tracks. You know what I mean? By the time I'm old, I want to be a grand dame with a mouth full of curses and plenty of cleavage.'

Dr Freeman was tapping the dangerous point of his pencil against his clipboard. 'Rosie,' he said, 'it would seem you deliberately misunderstood me. Shall we try again? I would like you to tell me what you dreamed, say, last night.' The technicolor green was flashing. I couldn't find my reflection in his eyes. He was making me his own, and my mother's hand at the other end of that thick rubber band was looking blue and lifeless. They had me.

'I dreamed . . .'

'Yes, Rosie. I'm listening.'

'Tell the doctor, Rosie.'

'I dreamed I was at the entrance of the twenty-four-hour supermarket where my mother shops by day, but never at night. Never at night.' My voice was slowing down in my head. It was gathering strange echoes and resonances. 'My face was pressed up against the big glass pane, and the whole store was lit up like some kind of fluorescent heaven. There were people there, too many people for the middle of the night. Something wasn't right. I – I was about to turn away when I realised that everyone was asleep, except me. Except me. Everyone was sleep-shopping.

'Then the automatic door opened by itself and I walked through. But I was so scared that I was going to wake some-one . . .'

'So what did you do, Rosie?'

'I slipped off my loafers so I wouldn't squeak, and shelved them with the day-old bread. I was heading for the meat-chiller when I saw the butcher with the blood on his apron.'

'Did he see you?'

'No – Yes – I'm not sure. You see, I jumped into the arms of a passing stock-boy and pretended I was his bride until I was safely past. Then I followed the cold breeze to the meat chiller.'

'What were you looking for, Rosie?'

'I wasn't sure, not at first. I crept past the lamb chops that bleated at me from the cold, and the chicken breasts with the silicon implants. That's when I saw them.'

'Saw what, Rosie? Tell me what you saw.'

'The cows' tongues. I could see them through the clouds of dry ice, silent on their styrofoam trays. Dozens of them. My hand was reaching for one. My mouth was watering. I felt the blue, wrinkled skin of the cellophane. I picked up the tray. Then the tip of that tongue began to wriggle and flex, and the cellophane started to rip.

'I tried to seal it up again. I tried to put it back. "They cut out my tongue!" it shrieked. "They called me a silly cow. A silly, silly cow!" The sleep-shoppers were waking up. The butcher was coming my way. I dropped the guilty tongue. I ran back to my stock-boy. I jumped into his arms. "Happy Anniversary, sweet stock-boy of mine!" I sang.

'That's all.' I looked up. I felt cold. Exposed. I had surrendered to Dr Freeman.

But there was no Dr Freeman. There was no mother. I stood up. I seemed to be alone with only the clipboard on the chair where Dr Freeman had been.

Then I saw them – on all fours in the shag-pile. Dr Freeman had dropped one of his contacts. The spell was broken.

'Right, Rosie,' he said with his one green eye. 'I think you've made some genuine progress here today. What do you think?'

I stuck out my tongue. Then I grabbed my mother's handbag, slung it over her arm, and pushed her, sobbing, out of the office, past Raquel, into the Shopping Village.

That night, in my sweet-teen bedroom, I received the gift of tongues.

The air was still and sticky-hot. The street lights cast bars of light through my Venetian blinds and across my bare arms and legs. I lay awake, listening to the blue electric sizzle of mosquitoes as they hit the bug-killer in our backyard. I couldn't sleep. I rolled over, twice. I pulled the sheet up, then off again. I turned myself wrong-side up, so that my feet rested on my pillow and my head lolled over the end of the bed I had outgrown. Blood rushed to my face. A bar of light caught me across the eyes and shattered into purple and gold as I closed them. I was thirsty. My tongue felt thick in my mouth. I thought about the glass of stale water on my night table, up at the other end of the bed, but I never made it. Before I could shift my feet from the pillow, I was bolt upright in bed and charged like some kind of lightning rod. My spine was rigid; my jaw locked. I tried to call out but couldn't. I didn't know what was happening.

I waited – for I don't know how long – my fists gripping the sheet. I waited for the awful hush that filled me up to break, to crack open, to let go of me. Something was pushing and swelling in the dark of my throat, like something wanting to be born, and I was scared.

Part of me was saying, this isn't happening – a ghost of a voice inside my head that I could hardly hear. It was saying whatever this is, it doesn't happen in the suburbs. I could hear a dog barking a few streets away, but I couldn't turn my head. I could hear the thrum of traffic from the distant highway, but I couldn't swallow. I wasn't myself. Not at all. And if I wasn't myself, who was I?

From the corner of my eye, I could just make out something in my bedroom mirror. Something flickering, purple and orange and yellow and blue. It was a single tongue of fire, sitting on the darkness like some wonderful illusion. For a moment, I forgot about everything: the sizzle of the mosquitoes and the charge between my vertebrae and the fearsome silence in my mouth. I just watched that wavering tongue of fire. It had started off small, but it was growing, feeding on the still air. It was the size of a flame-eater's meal when I smelled hair, my hair, burning. That flame was hovering just over my head.

I grabbed my pillow. That's what I remember next – my arms moving again, and my voice yelling 'Fire!', and the power of my own voice almost winding me. But the fire wouldn't be put out.

The fire chief told my father we were lucky. 'Mostly smoke damage,' he said. 'Could have been worse.'

My father was still rubbing his eyes. He looked like a man trapped in someone else's dream. 'What – how did it happen?'

'Well, we're investigating, sir, but if you want my opinion . . .'

'I do. Please.'

'Looks to me like a case of a faulty teenage girl, somewhere I'd say between the ages of twelve and sixteen. I've seen it before.'

I left the shelter of the garage where my mother and I were huddling in our nightgowns. I ran into the driveway, pushing myself between father and fire chief. 'That's me,' I breathed. 'The girl – between twelve and sixteen.' My father hardly looked at me; it was all too clear who I was. 'I can explain every –'

'You've gotta be careful,' said the fire chief, ignoring me. 'They're touchy as touch-paper at this age. Anything can set them off.'

'But it wasn't like that!' I cried.

Breakfast was burnt toast and sausages. My mother was crying again. My father told her it was time for the priest.

It was a little cramped for two in the confessional, but my mother insisted. She stood with her back to the door and prompted me.

'Forgive me, Father, for I have sinned,' I repeated.

'Yes, Rosie,' came the voice of Father Pater from the other side of the little velvet curtain. Anonymity was unheard of in our town. 'What is it you would like to confess?'

Silence.

And more silence. My mother kicked my ankle.

'I stink of smoke. Three guesses.'

'I did hear about the fire last night, Rosie. Were you smoking in bed again?'

I hesitated. 'Do you want the truth?'

'Of course I want the truth.'

'I was speaking in tongues.'

My mother bit her lip.

Father Pater paused. 'I see.'

'No. You don't. I can tell.' The air in the confessional was stale and warm. Sweat was gathering on my forehead. I was trying to breathe. 'There was this voice. In my throat.

And there was a flame – above my head. A tongue of fire. Real – fire.'

Father Pater inhaled loudly. He was taking my air. 'Well, if that is the case, Rosie, do you know what this means?'

'No – No – I don't.' I was starting to hyperventilate.

'It means hell-fire. It just might mean possession. In short, it means you've been a naughty girl.'

'And her penance, Father?' asked my mother, chiming in.

'Well, it's debatable, of course, but I've always said, mortify the flesh, save the soul.'

'BUT I'M STILL DEVELOPING!' I screamed. I got to my feet and heaved on the door, sending my mother flying into a pile of hymnals outside. A pair of altar-boys whistled as I ran out of the church, gulping for air.

I ran and I ran as fast as I could. I ran until I made it to Buddy's Ice-Cream Parlour on the edge of town. Buddy Junior, who lived on the wrong side of the old railway tracks, was scooping ice-cream.

'Make it a double, Buddy,' I panted.

'Sure thing, Rosie.' I watched his muscle scurry up and down his arm as he carved out two scoops of passion fruit. He smiled at me through the glass. 'You're looking really hot today, Rosie.'

'I ran all the way here.'

'Glad to hear it. This one's on the house.'

I smiled back and took a seat on one of the spinning stools at the counter. Then I licked my passion fruit cone clean round its creamy circumference. Buddy leaned across the counter. 'They tell me you can catch flies with that tongue of yours, Rosie.' I didn't look up. 'They tell me you're fast.'

I went on licking my cone. 'Maybe.'

'"Maybe" isn't what I heard.'

'No,' I said. 'Maybe's what I'm saying. And I'll say no more, Buddy Wannamaker Junior, until I finish my cone.'

Buddy shuffled on his feet and sulked. 'But that cone's a double-whammy.'

I licked a dollop of passion fruit off the end of my nose with the tip of my tongue.

'Rosie, you're making me crazy.'

I finished in my own good time. Then I spun round languorously on my stool a few times. At last I said, 'All right, Buddy. You can kiss me.'

Buddy leaped over the counter.

My tongue was a wonder in his mouth. It moved like no other. It ran circles round his. It did somersaults, backwards and forwards. For a little while, it danced the rumba. Then it disappeared in a game of hide-and-seek. Finally, it reappeared and did a loop-the-loop in mid-air. Buddy was the first boy I had met who could hold his breath for as long as me.

We might have been there for hours if my mother hadn't walked in. 'Rosie, you will take your tongue out of that boy's mouth this instant!'

Buddy leaped back over the counter and hid.

'How could you, Rosie? How could you just run off like that? I've broken a heel just trying to catch up with you.' She took a seat on the stool next to mine and started spinning round dolefully. For a little while, neither of us spoke.

Then my mother let out a great sigh and slumped over the Formica counter. 'Rosie, I have not said this yet, but I am saying it now. I am at a loss. I am at an absolute loss. You have stuck your tongue out at a doctor. You have set fire to your father's house. And you have bedevilled our own parish priest. I just don't know what to do with you anymore. How Rosie – can you tell me this? – *How* do you expect me to go on shopping in this town?'

I said I didn't know. Buddy appeared from behind the milkshake machine and said he didn't know either. My mother and I both spun on our stools for a little while longer, then I said, 'Mom, do you want me to go to live with Bill and Ida in Labrador? Would that make things easier?'

'No, you foolish girl, I do not want you to go live with Bill and Ida in Labrador. I just want – and this is all I want – I just want you to learn to hold that tongue of yours until you're twenty-one. Is that too much for a mother to ask?'

I looked at my mother's pressed lips.

I looked at Buddy Junior's wide, worried eyes.

'No, of course that's not too much to ask.' Even as I spoke, my tongue nestled cosily in my cheek.

The
Fallen
Warrior

.

MIRIAM BURKE

It's a Thursday morning, and like every Thursday my body wakes me at dawn. It knows what's in store for it and wants as many hours as possible of the sweetness of anticipated pleasure. I open the curtain and look out at the rain dancing jigs on the wet road under the street-light. The mail train passes behind and the house trembles. I stand at the window, dreaming of him, until the winter sun routs the darkness.

I have a bath and shave carefully. I put on a new white shirt I got in Dunnes and dither a while about which sports jacket to wear. He usually arrives soon after I get back from work, so there'll be no time to change. I try not to look at my face as I shave. The broken veins have created an alarming similarity between it and an ordnance survey map of the country. And my teeth are like a crowd of men at a bar at closing time, all bunched together with the odd one pushed out in front of the others. A few forlorn strands of grey hair stretch across the barren scalp. My ears are my best feature, small with well-defined contours. They look like fine porcelain or sea shell.

I go down to the kitchen, put tea bags in the pot and cornflakes in a bowl. The fridge is bereft of milk so it's Lough Derg tea and dry flakes. It is still raining and I get soaked on the walk to work. I'd left the umbrella the night before at one of the stations of the cross, McDaids probably. I decide to surrender myself to the rain, and throw back my head. The great warrior Ferdia wouldn't have cowered under a few drops of rain. I am taking the First Years for Geography at nine, so I give a few minutes' attention to what I might do with them. There is time for a cup of tea in the staff room before class. I am sitting reading the *Irish Times* when Maighread rushes in and sits opposite me. 'Ah, Padraigh, it's yourself that's in it. Are you coming with us on the Abortion March on Saturday?'

'No,' I say, and shove the paper up so that it eclipses my face.

She leans across the table and pushes her face into the front page. 'Padraigh, you can't believe that the slaughter of young children is a good thing?'

'I think it's a great thing. I only wish we could raise the age limit to cover my First Year Geography Class.'

'May God forgive you Padraigh O'Brien, making fun of such serious matters. It's that Protestant newspaper that's corrupting your soul.'

A few more colleagues have come in, so she goes over to work on them.

I leave the staff room and walk towards the classroom. I see Caitlin Boyle at the other end of the corridor walking in my direction. Her blush has travelled to her neck by the time we meet.

'Good morning, Miss Boyle. And how are you this wet day?'

'I'm fine, thank you, Mr O'Brien. And how is your mother?' she says quietly.

'She's picked up a bit. I'll go down again this weekend.'

'It's a long old journey to County Clare. You're a wonderful son Mr O'Brien.'

'I must be getting along. You know what a terrible hunger for learning the First Years have, Miss Boyle, it wouldn't do to be late.'

'Goodbye Mr O'Brien.'

She'll spend the rest of the day going over this conversation and dreaming, as she has for twenty years, of the day I'll invite her to the Teatime Express.

As I walk to the classroom, I think of him, running in his coltish way down O'Connell Street, late for work. Tucking in his shirt at the back, his black curls dancing, and a fag hanging from the side of his mouth. My Cuchullain. Eight and a half more hours. Even the sullenness of thirty adolescents can't touch me today. As I walk into the classroom I give Duffy what I hope is an intimidating look. A look that says 'Don't push your luck'. The week before he had greeted me with 'Mr O'Brien, will you tell us why you never married?'

'Because I had a premonition that I might have a freak like you for a son, Duffy.'

His mates sniggered behind him. I was awake all night

trying to remember if anyone could have seen me going into the sauna.

At lunch-time I slip out to the pub for two pints and a cheese sandwich. I take the paper to ward off the other drinkers. I close my eyes to see his supple white body, and I plan how I will pay homage to it. My mouth moving all over him until he screams for release. Our bodies moving together and the wildness of him when he comes. Four more hours.

It's Second Year Maths after lunch. They seem to think a man must be able to teach Maths. I didn't like to point out that I had failed Intercert Maths. I hadn't got around to preparing the lesson so we do a mathematical appraisal of the Lotto. This leads to much merriment. McCarthy says he will hire a demolition crew to flatten the school if he wins. Someone else says they'll bribe their way to being Taoiseach and ban all education. He's sitting at his desk now, filing cheques or touching a keyboard with his elegant long fingers.

I'd run home if a middle aged man running wasn't such an alarming sight. I drop into the Off Licence to pick up a bottle of Black Bush. I'm home by five-fifteen; he usually arrives about five-thirty. I sit in the living room, the *Evening Herald* open on my lap, and a glass of Black Bush in my hand. I can be seen from the short path that leads to the front door. I notice my hand is shaking. When he hasn't arrived by six-thirty I know he's not just late. He can't have got the day wrong because it's been every Thursday for two years. I decide to get completely plastered. I know I'm storing up terrible suffering for the following morning, but it'll be a distraction.

The neat whisky cauterises the raging wound. By the time

half the bottle is drunk, everything is grand again. We had great times and the memories won't abandon me. And sure maybe he'll come next week and tell me he had to go to a relative's funeral in the country. I'm fit for anything by the end of the bottle. Ireland is full of lads with black curls and winning ways. Maybe tomorrow night I'll find another. I trip on the stairs and give my head a wallop. I sleep in my clothes and shoes. I wake at dawn. I have the mother and father of a headache. I avoid the bathroom mirror and go down to the kitchen to make tea. I drink a cup and then throw up in the kitchen sink. Fifteen minutes of dry retching follows. Sometimes green bile comes up. I'm frightened of what else will come up. I find myself crying. Jesus fucking Christ, hell couldn't be worse than this. At least there would be other sinners there, and there are some very fetching pictures of Lucifer.

I summon the courage to look in the bathroom mirror. There's a lump the size of a sliotar on my forehead, and no hair to camouflage it. I lie on the bed and wait for it all to abate. At nine I telephone the school and tell them I have severe food poisoning from a take-away chicken. I leave the house at twelve and have a medicinal two pints in the nearest pub. They do the trick, thank God. I continue on to one of my usual haunts.

'Good afternoon Mr O'Brien. You must have had a good night.'

'I did, Pascal, until I was attacked by a vicious stairs, and in my own house at that.'

'They're terrible dangerous things them stairs, you need to keep your eye on them at all times.'

I take my pint to a table and a thirsty poet joins me. I buy him a pint and a chaser, because he looks in even worse shape than me.

A few pints later and I set off for the sauna. There's always a priest or a married man there with their tongue hanging out for it. I go to the steam room. My tears can't be seen as some shadowy figure rams me from behind. I leave quickly, checking to see if there are any boys hanging around outside. It's another wet day. I pass a group of tinkers fighting outside an undertaker's. Their children cower in a doorway nearby. I walk down Moore Street Market. I avoid looking at the women's faces, not wanting to see the anger and disappointment in them. I walk around for an hour and then find myself at my destination, not knowing I had one.

It's an empty lounge bar, with ripped plastic seats. A Country and Western song is coming through the sound-system. The carpet is sticky from spilled beer and the men's toilet is about as bad as I've seen. The barman is from the Liberties and is suspicious of anyone with a country accent like mine. He thinks I might be with the Special Branch. There are Sinn Fein posters on the walls. The top half of the window is clear glass and I sit where I can comfortably see out. I'm drinking a brandy and port now, I couldn't face another pint. I look at the paper until five. Then I watch the door of the bank. Dozens of them step out. More girls than boys. Fresh, giddy young things. He's one of the last. My heart moves at the sight of his lovely head. I feel no surprise when I see there is a girl with him. She has long dark hair and moves gracefully. They walk down the street together. As he reaches for her hand, I feel a spear run through my heart.

Out of Darkness

.

DEBORAH MOFFAT

I like it here, in this church. I like the polished floor-boards that gleam in the morning sun. I like the plain white walls. I like the ceiling, which is pale blue, the colour of the sky in winter. Most of all I like the light in here. There is light everywhere, all around me, the clear white light of day, streaming in through the high, narrow windows. I like it here because of the light. Because there is light, I know that this is a holy place, because God is light. I know about God from the pictures I've seen, on the walls at the Pearsons' house. In those pictures, God stands in heaven, parting the dark clouds that cover the earth to let great pillars of light beam down on us here below. A halo of light crowns His head. Light shines down on us from heaven, and when there is light, God is there.

Because the church is light and clean and bright, it looks big, bigger than it really is. I feel small, small and alone, as if I were sitting on this long, hard pew all by myself. I wish I were all by myself. When God looks down at me, when God sees me here, I want Him to see me by myself, all alone. I don't want Him to think that I belong to the people that are sitting here with me. These people, the Pearsons, have nothing to do with me. They are just taking care of me, just for the weekend, because my mother is away. That's why I'm here in this church, because the Pearsons have brought me with them. Whenever I stay with them, they bring me to church. When I'm at home, I don't go to church. My mother doesn't believe in it, and anyway, she's never up this early on a Sunday.

The minister is talking, reading something from the Bible. I'm not really paying attention to what he's saying. I only listen sometimes, when I hear a word or a phrase that I like, when the minister says something that fits the idea that I have of God. But I don't really think that God is in the words the minister uses, or in a book, in the Bible. I think He's here, in the church, in the light streaming in through the windows. He's in the air, in here and outside and everywhere, in the air we breathe and in the clear sky up above and in the bright light sparkling outside on the snow. Wherever there's light, there is God.

There is no light at the Pearsons' house. Their windows are covered with layers of dirty plastic film to keep the cold out, and their rooms are cramped with big, heavy furniture, and there are clothes hanging everywhere to dry. The cast-iron stove in the kitchen leaks blue smoke and grey ash all through the house. The Pearsons rise before dawn, and the men – Mr Pearson and the hired hands – work outside all day long, doing chores around the farm or logging out in the woods, until dark. At breakfast and at supper, they all sit around the kitchen table, drinking black tea and grumbling about the hard work they do. Mrs Pearson tells me don't be lazy, get up and clear the table. As I go round lifting up the plates, the hired men make fun of me, teasing me in their deep, gravelly voices. Their faces are burned red, their teeth stained brown, their hands black with grime. I'm sure they are evil, but Mrs Pearson says that they're all God-fearing Christians, not like some people she could name.

As we are leaving church she asks me why I wasn't singing along with the hymns. The truth is, I don't like it when everyone stands up to sing. I get buried in the darkness, lost in the crush of bodies swaying high above me. I can't see the light, can't see God, and He can't see me. Anyway, I don't know the words of the hymns, so how can I sing them? That's what I tell Mrs Pearson: that I don't know the words.

She says, 'Well, can't you read, Lucy? A big girl like you, ten years old, can't even *read*? I thought you were supposed to be so smart!'

Sometimes she tells me I'm too smart for my own good, or she tells me not to be a little smarty-pants. Other times she wonders why I can't do certain things, like sew or cook or iron clothes, if I'm supposed to be so smart. 'My own girls could do that at half your age,' she tells me.

'Weren't you singing?' Mr Pearson asks me now, about the hymns. 'Maybe you thought God wasn't listening to you. But He was; He was listening, and wondering why you weren't singing!'

'For heaven's sake, don't fill her head with notions!' Mrs Pearson scolds her husband. 'She has enough silly ideas as it is.' To me she says, 'God doesn't pay special attention to *you*, Miss. He only cares about good little girls.'

After church, I can go home. Mr Pearson has to take me in his truck. The seats are covered with dust and stained with grease. We bounce along over the icy road, going slowly, so slowly I'm afraid I'll never get home. When Mr Pearson finally pulls up to our house, I jump right out and run to the door, without saying goodbye or thank you or anything. I just want to get away from Mr Pearson and his dirty old truck.

In our house, there is both light and dark, depending on how my mother is feeling. Today, it's dark. All the curtains are closed, and my mother is in bed. 'Ooooh, my head hurts,' she groans, when I go upstairs to tell her I'm home. 'Be an angel and bring me some water. Mummy doesn't feel well.' I bring her some water and she tells me to go away and be quiet.

She stays in bed most of the day. When she gets up, she doesn't get dressed. She sits in the dark, staring at the flickering light of the television, drinking rum and coke. Her hair is dirty, and black make-up is smudged all around her eyes. She won't talk to me, won't let me put on the light, snaps at me when I make too much noise. I tip-toe upstairs to my room, get into bed and pull the covers over my head, hiding from the evil that's trapped inside our dark house.

One morning, when I go downstairs, the curtains are all pulled back and the rooms are blazing with sunlight. My mother is dressed for housework, in faded blue-jeans and an old flannel shirt, her hair pulled away from her face in a tight pony-tail. She's throwing open all the windows, letting in fresh air, clearing out the dust, the dirt, the musty old smells. She changes the beds, washes our clothes, and then I help her hang the laundry out on the line. When our work is done, my mother releases her hair from the pony-tail and it floats out like a bright cloud around her head. We sit together on the front step, tilting our faces up to the sun; she says she's trying to get some colour into our pale cheeks, but I know that we're praying, smiling up at God who's smiling down at us.

In the evening, my mother tells me that I have to spend the night at the Pearsons' because she's going out on a date. 'It's just for one night,' she promises me. That's what she always says, but sometimes she calls up the Pearsons the next morning and asks them to keep me for another day, or even longer. Tonight she gets all dressed up before I have to go. She puts on a dark-blue dress, and lots of gold jewellery, and she combs her hair so that it flows long and straight down either side of her face. I think she looks beautiful when she's all ready to go out; she looks just like Mary, in the pictures on the walls at the Pearsons' house.

In summer, my mother goes away and doesn't come back.

At the Pearsons', I'm supposed to help with the chores. My mother gave them some money before she went away, but not enough to pay for my bed and board, Mr Pearson says. 'And it's not as if that woman couldn't afford any more,' Mrs Pearson complains. She says to me, 'You'll just have to get used to hard work, Miss High and Mighty. You'll get your hands dirty this summer!'

In the morning and in the evening there's milking in the barn. All day long there's cleaning and cooking in the house, or weeding out in the garden. I don't want to work inside, in the house or in the barn, hidden away in the darkness when the sun is shining so brightly outside. I don't mind being out in the garden, but I can't do what Mrs Pearson tells me to do. She wants me to pull up the little weeds growing around the vegetables, but how can I destroy what God has made grow? The work is hard, and there's no point in it – the weeds will just grow again, anyway. When Mrs Pearson isn't looking, I run away to the woods and lie down in the long grass under the trees. Golden drops of light shine down through the green leaves and fall on the ground where I lie. I know that God is in every one of those drops of light.

In September, my mother comes back and I go home. But home is different now: there's a man living here with us. His name is Jeff. He tells me that my name, Lucy, means light. He's always telling me things like that – the meaning of words and the names of things around us. He points to flowers and trees and birds, and tells me what they're called. One day he gives me a book that names all the birds in North America. I say 'thank you' and flip through the book, admiring the pictures, and then I put it aside. I don't really care about the names of the birds, or about any of the other information in the book. I like the mystery of not knowing, of not understanding the world around me. I'm sure that everything I need to know will be revealed to me by God, in good time. He will lead me out of darkness, into light.

But Jeff is puzzled. 'Can't Lucy read?' he asks my

mother. 'I was watching her when she looked through that book; all she did was look at the pictures!'

'Yeah,' my mother says, yawning. 'She reads. Maybe she's kind of rusty at it, or something. She probably didn't read much all summer.' She sighs. 'It's those people I left her with, the Pearsons. They're stupid, ignorant people. I'll bet they don't even have a book in the house.'

'They do so,' I tell her. 'The Bible.'

The Pearsons don't need books. They already know all of the things they'll ever need to know. They do the same thing every day, just like they've always done, like their parents and grandparents did before them. They don't allow anything or anyone to change or interrupt their routine. They always say that they run their own lives, that nobody is going to tell them what to do. They like to think that their cows produce milk, and their fields grow crops, and their chickens lay eggs, all because of the hard work that they do. They don't want to leave anything to God; they have to do it all themselves.

I think Jeff is just the same as them. He wants to rule his world, the world around him, with his books, his words, his names for things. He wants control; he wants to control us.

Mr Pearson says that's what my mother needs: a man to tame her, somebody to control her. 'She always was pretty wild,' he says, winking across the table at me. 'Just like you, Lucy. Always running away.'

I'm staying at the Pearsons' again, because my mother and Jeff are going out somewhere tonight. At supper, the hired men tease me. 'How do you like your new daddy?' one of them asks me.

'Shh, shh!' Mrs Pearson hushes them. 'He's not her daddy! Those two aren't even married.' She looks down at me over her steaming cup of bitter tea. 'This poor child never even knew her real father.'

I keep my mouth shut, but I want to say: I don't need a Daddy. God is my Father.

On Sunday afternoon, when I get home, my mother is still in bed and all the curtains are drawn. Jeff says my mother isn't feeling well; she had too much to drink the night before, he explains. 'I'm not at all happy about her drinking,' he says. 'I'm going to make her quit. She has got to stop, or she'll kill herself.'

I want to tell him it's not up to him, what she does; it's not even up to her. God runs our lives, and we live according to His will. But in the sour darkness of the house I know that my mother doesn't live according to God's will, not anymore; she has gone astray.

Jeff says that the best thing for her – for all of us – is to go out for a walk in the fresh air, and for once I agree with him. I think that if we can all get outdoors, out into the clear grey light of the cold November day, God will look down and see us, and He will deliver us from Evil.

Together, we beg my mother to get dressed, to come downstairs and go out for a walk with us. In the end she agrees, although by then it's late in the afternoon, not long before dark. We bundle up in our coats and start off, Jeff leading the way. Almost immediately, my mother says she wishes she hadn't come with us. Jeff makes us walk fast, and says he intends to go far. We carry on, my mother complaining and lagging behind and stopping every so often to catch her breath. 'I feel sick!' she warns Jeff. 'Let's go back.' She looks sick; her face is kind of yellow and her eyes are all puffy and swollen. Jeff says the only thing wrong with her is that she's hungover. The best thing for a hangover, he insists, is exercise. 'So get moving,' he orders my mother.

I don't like the way they talk to each other. They're always arguing. I run ahead to get away from them, so I won't have to hear what they're saying. Running, I lose track of the path we've been following, and when I look for it, I can't find it anywhere. I'm lost, but I don't mind. I'm sure that God will show me the way.

I raise my eyes, looking for Him, waiting for Him to guide me. The sky is cloudy and dark. I can only just see the sun, pale and white behind the clouds, hanging low in the sky, near the horizon. I climb towards the top of the hill, aiming for the sun. As I walk, the clouds separate, and now the sun crowns the hill-top with a bright blaze of flaming orange light.

Just ahead of me, I see the fire-tower, rising up into the sky, tall and thin and narrowing at the top like the steeple of the Pearsons' church. The metal frame glows gold in the low light of the setting sun. I've seen the fire-tower before, but only from a distance. I know what it is, and why it's here. My mother has told me all about it, how it was built so that the forest rangers could climb up high and see out over the hills, watching for signs of fire in these forests. I want to climb the tower, but not because I want to look down at the woods below me; I want to get as high as I can, to be closer to God. I want to stand at the top of the tower, offering myself to God. I want to raise my arms to Him, to be lifted up to the kingdom of glory in heaven above.

I hear voices. Jeff and my mother are calling my name. I start to climb the tower stairs. When I get up to the first landing, I look down. I can see Jeff and my mother, running through the woods, coming over to the tower. 'There she is!' Jeff points his finger at me. 'I'm coming after you, Lucy,' he yells. 'Beat you to the top!'

My mother leans against a tree. 'Oh, be careful, you two!' she cries. 'That looks dangerous.'

'You come too,' I say to her.

'No way, honey. It's too high. I can't.'

'Please!' I beg her. She has to come; she can't stay down there on the ground, all by herself. She'll be left behind when God comes for us. If only she'd try to climb the stairs, we could all rise together – my mother, and me, and Jeff too – to God's kingdom in the sky.

'Oh, come on,' Jeff urges her. 'It's not that high.'

My mother shudders. 'No, Jeff. I said no!' She sinks to the ground, sits with her back against the tree. 'It makes me dizzy just looking at you two up there.'

'Okay, okay, forget it.' Jeff starts climbing. 'Hurry up, Lucy,' he calls out. 'I'm catching up with you.'

I climb as fast as I can. I don't want to let Jeff get past me, can't let him be the first to reach the top. The stairs get steeper and narrower as I climb, and they turn round and round on themselves in a tight spiral, so that my head is spinning when I get to the little platform at the top. I sit down on the floor for a moment, too tired to look around. I can't see anything but the sky, anyway, from where I'm sitting, because the platform has sides, little low walls about two feet high, too high for me to see over.

When I hear Jeff getting close to the platform, his footsteps pounding loud on the stairs just below me, I scramble over to the side on my knees, and peer over the wall, looking down. Right away, I wish I hadn't. I feel sick, weak with disappointment. I've climbed so high, as high as I possibly can, but I'm still so close to the earth, so far from Heaven! The ground below seems to swell up towards me, and then to fade back in waves of darkness.

My mother jumps up, screaming. 'Honey, watch out! Don't lean over the edge like that! Jeff, hold on to her! Oh, be *careful*, you guys!'

'Will you shut *up*?' Jeff mutters, standing beside me. He raises his voice, calling down to my mother, 'For Christ's sake, she's perfectly safe up here!'

But I don't feel safe. I feel as if I'm already falling. God doesn't want me, doesn't see me here, won't help me. I can climb as high as I want, but He won't care. There is no saving grace in high places, in the clear light of day, in all my silly notions about God.

I throw up over the side of the platform.

Jeff grunts, and steps back. 'Some people just don't have a head for heights,' he says.

As we walk back to the house, my mother and Jeff start arguing again. My mother says she deserves a drink after all this; Jeff says she doesn't. I trail along behind them, collecting dead leaves. When I get home, I'll ask Jeff to show me a book about trees. I need to know the names of things.

Before the
Power Cuts
Started

.

CATHY NADEN

Eugenie and Paul jump when the shots are fired, faces hidden behind a cushion. When they peep out the credits are rolling. It's dark outside the large french windows. It's dark in the room, the only light from the TV and the old anglepoise.

Eugenie, still holding the cushion, goes out to the hallway, through to the kitchen, but finds the door is locked. There has been a bolt on this door for years, one of those cheap ones from the Hollybush Store, but no one's ever used it till now. Eugenie contemplates the shut door with her small intense eyes, hand half ready to knock. Mrs Bliss is talking low and adult-talk on the other side, but Eugenie can't make out any words above the rain which hasn't let up all day. She rejoins her brother in the sitting room, puts the cushion on his lap, and rests her head there. She tries to follow what Robert MacDougall is saying on the news, but after nine o'clock TV speaks a different language. Her thoughts are mussed up with what they did that day. Their hideout by the transmitter tower was wet. In the mud they marked out boundaries with sticks. London, a supermarket and a war. The afternoon they spent burying things they'd lifted from the house like broken teacups, action man, her dead fish which died today, pieces of paper from the red cupboard drawer.

Paul leans forward to change channels, knocking her head off the cushion. She kicks the air with her dirty lace-ups, annoyed at the disturbance. Paul finds one of those nature programmes with pictures of planets and talking:

> . . . It is generally believed that life on Earth began on the Earth itself, sometime after the formation of the planets between four and five thousand million years ago. But it is also suggested life was deposited here from Outer Space . . .

Eugenie is humming bored. Space makes her think of books. She examines Paul while he watches. His face is blue and twitching with TV reflections of stars, but she can still make out the same pointy nose, the same round face, the same dark eyes as hers. Everyone called them peas in a pod. But she has other ideas.

'I'm not your real sister,' she says. Paul responds by not answering, but this doesn't put her off. 'I'm a changeling. You know what that is?'

Paul folds his arms so they stick out at right angles.

'It means your real sister was taken away and I was put in her place. That's why we look so alike, so no one will guess.'

Paul doesn't like the way the streetlight stabs at him through the big gap in the curtains, nor his sister's hot baby-breath in the dark, whispering goddamn lies again. It seems unlikely that some bollocking fairies have stolen away the real Eugenie and replaced her with this replica. Eugenie talks herself to sleep, unbothered by the cars on the streets outside and the voices floating through from the kitchen. Now she is safely in girl's sleep, Paul steals a look at her for signs of dreaming. Wonders if his sister's dormant face might yield some secret of her true origins. Maybe there is some tell-tale difference that can't be seen or touched, which'll only be revealed as time goes by.

Friday night, March 1969. They are two small shadows in a cast of thousands. Mr and Mrs Bliss are the stars; remote, tall and experienced, bombed-out on TV moon landings and experimental love. They bathe Eugenie and Paul in the mornings, take them to the bus-stop, call them in before the six o'clock ghosts, and instruct them that nothing matters more in life than the pursuit of happiness.

Other people around: Bob and Sue; the Costello Family; lodgers Dixon, who leaves curly hairs in the bath and plays a trumpet, and peroxide Joan; also Adrian and Nicky, the paper-factory sons; Paulette the French woman; and Pip, who people take advantage of. Then there are visitors who come for an hour and stay much longer. Patricia, lost in love, sleeps on a mattress in one of the spare rooms. Beverley, in her open-topped car, brought a daisy tree which still stands in the corner of the hall unplanted. There are some famous people too, actors from adverts, trainee journalists, campaigners and left-wing politicians.

Behind the kitchen door Mrs Bliss is having a bad night. Worse than usual. Must be the rain. She keeps sobbing: 'Who'd be out on a night like this?' Pulling the blinds down over the windows and letting them snap open again almost immediately, as if she's seen something in the street outside.

Across the other side of the city a black taxi cab pulls up outside a large terraced house on a leafy suburban road. The driver is mid-thirties but looks younger. Slim, almost too thin for his height, which is tall. Looks like he's lost weight rather than naturally this way. His passenger is a young woman, wearing a headscarf with roses on it. He leaves the engine running, jumps out, and joins her on the back seat. Even in that short dash from front to back the rain has caught his shirt, leaving strange dark spots like sweat.

'Tomorrow . . . yes?' she falters in bad English.

'Saturday. I don't know . . . yes.' He is conscious that he is picking up her strange intonations and kisses her.

She gets out, walks up the path without turning back. She walks slowly, her neat hands turned slightly upwards as if feeling the wet, as if she can't quite believe any of it is real.

He watches her fumble with the lock. Tries to put himself in her shoes. How weird it must be to come to a new land and half-speak the language. Then he drives off. Around. Driving in the same rain Mrs Bliss is trying to shut out.

Mrs Bliss pours a whisky and tunes the radio to long wave for the chatter of foreign stations and tries not to think how her life has burst, silently, like a pillow. She longs for comprehension. The cars go by all the time and she's gripped with this fear that one of them might stop and rescue her. A strange world of absence, this. Make no mistake. Everything looks the same, but somebody, somewhere, is playing tricks on her senses. Magic is at work. She leafs through the *Yellow Pages*, looking for names of private detectives. The wall where the phone is fixed has numbers scrawled all over it in different coloured biro; wonky felt-tip pen lines mark out heights over the years: mum, dad, E, P, cat, dog. Mrs Bliss thinks if she painted the kitchen she could erase quite a lot, disconnect numbers from the past.

The rain, which had eased off, starts to fall heavily against the windows, scrambling her momentary peace. Wet car drives by. Was that a woman's voice, low from the other side of the wall? Another car, stalling. Two more further away. The rain and engines and puddle splash on tarmac make her insides collide. Will the next car stop outside the house? It's pissing it down. She's never heard such a busy chattering sound. A mess of morse-code bleeps and chips in hot oil. The house is jumping. Electric clicks, radiator pops, stair carpet thuds, ceiling creaks. This is just the tip of the iceberg, these noises poltergeisting her home. There are other things: doors closing as she approaches, long auburn hairs, Nina Ricci perfume, secret smiles, the yellow roses bought on Tuesday, phone calls, TV messages, and cars with dark windows casing the street. She wants her whole crap life investigated, starting with Mr Bliss.

She goes back to thumbing the *Yellow Pages* and finds the name Perry, Private Detective. She scores under the entry with her wedding ring finger, the only one with a decent nail.

Her senses are razor-sharp, tight with whisky and waiting. It's no ordinary waiting either. She's not hanging on for Mr Bliss to get back. Shit, no. This is something else. She feels animal-alert, like something is about to happen. A call from a past love, a stranger caught in the rain looking for shelter, a police raid, cops crawling over the house, arresting everything in sight from the lodgers to the pets. Taking her husband away for his copycat crimes of the heart. She loses her train of thought and looks at the phone for a prompt.

Nothing happens. She spills a little whisky as she tops up her glass. Takes a sip. Remembers she hasn't put the bowl back under the skylight leak when she emptied it earlier. And then the phone rings.

She shouldn't be surprised, but she is. Her body stiffens. Is there magic at work? Is her very presence in this room, in this street, in this world, attracting and multiplying coincidences and chance and luck?

'Hello?' It's a man, American accent. 'Hi, it's Bob, calling from Canada. Did I wake you?'

Of course it's the wrong number, but he chats on for a while, full of transatlantic charm and ease, then casuals a goodbye and is gone. Mrs Bliss hesitates to hang up, balances the receiver in her palm, like it's *covered* in fingerprints. Come to think of it, she hates it when strangers puncture her life. Now she's dreaming of the rockies, which of course she's never seen.

The phone won't ring again. She hangs up. The whole city is nervous with rain. She curls up on the tired lino floor and falls asleep. Behind her brilliant but misguided eyes, pictures unfold of new events.

Mr Bliss, taxi driver by day, filmmaker by night, wakes up early. He crept in late last night. Hovered by the kitchen where, through the half-open door, he could see his wife stretched out.

Today it's British Summertime and unusually hot. He turns the clock an hour forward to eight-fifteen and rifles the wardrobe for some shorts. The sun falls across his eyes and illuminates his busy thoughts. He has one leg longer than the other, which causes back-pain. He has a bad memory, he has high blood pressure, he has a sore throat, he has an unidentified pain in his kidneys which comes and goes, he is free of it today, he has twenty-twenty vision, he has a con-stant craving for sex, he wishes he was a doctor but medicine is too vast to come to grips with. Best stick with what you know, always stick within a mapped-out life. Why sleep on a mattress on the floor? All their friends are doing it. He picks up Tuesday's paper from the floor of the bog and reads the article on Wilson again.

When he gets down to the kitchen, Saturday morning is underway. Mrs Bliss is topping up glasses of milk. Eugenie and Paul are talking over Marmite sandwiches.

'I hit him in the belly and kneed him in the face. Four of us on to two. They're younger than us and smaller and frightened, you can see it in their eyes.'

'I got dreams,' says Eugenie. 'I got dreams about super-acrobats. I got dreams about spinning round and high kicks.' She karate-chops the air. Something was born in her, making her uncertain, turning hugs into strangles.

'Dad,' says Paul, noticing him for the first time. 'You gonna fix it today?' Paul likes it when Mr Bliss fixes things.

He wants to be a mechanic, get in there, fuck around and fix things. Fix things for good so they never come apart again.

Mr Bliss looks out onto the paved front garden, where the edges of stone are still dark with wet in the bright sunshine. How did it get to be the weekend so soon? He has to work.

'There's money to be earned and things to be learned,' he says in an upbeat sixties' style. The best way to exercise authority is to leave the room, so he does.

Eugenie and Paul run off to play knives. The lodgers start trickling into the kitchen, preparing breakfast and talking wildly about politics and art. Mrs Bliss is not alone.

Across the other side of London, amongst the Polish exiles, Marian looks at photos of the family she left behind. She records letters to send them on a crappy old tape recorder her room-mate lent her, reading out bits of her horoscope from a magazine to show how her English is coming along: Everyone has something or someone to worry about . . . She hesitates over her pronunciation . . . Some corner of the mind which is never completely at ease or at rest. However, accept what cannot be changed this month.

Mr Bliss is out driving again. He dropped his first fare, an Australian air stewardess, at a hotel in Victoria and was hailed down moments later on Buckingham Palace Road. He hoped they would ask for a destination in North London, but the bloke wanted a restaurant in Balham he'd never heard of. He's not a taxi driver who talks a lot. What did he think about when he drove around? How many friends did he have? Did he prefer checked shirts or plain? How did his father die? What was his favourite drink? How much did he weigh? How long had he lived at number four, Macklin

Street? How often did he buy new underwear? What was his most frequented place? What happened at La Finca that night he got so drunk? Where was he when JFK got shot? How did he meet Marian? Which did he value more, self-confidence or fragility? What was the best sex he ever had? Did he go for a walk last thing at night to the Shell garage and back? Did he privilege men over women? Was he really only interested in people with connections? What were the five questions he wrote down on a piece of paper, aged nineteen, and still hadn't answered? Did he notice the way his hands shook, gentle as static? How exhilarated was he when he lost his way in the dark short cuts of backstreet London? How tall was he? Why did he stop being Mr Funny overnight? Was he aware of coincidences in his life? Why was loyalty such a big thing with him? What had led him to take this job? Did his passengers assume he had done nothing else? Did it bother Mr Bliss he was no good at small-talk? Did he know he occupied a special place in his wife's heart? How many hours did he spend watching TV? Did he like order in his life? Which living person, if any, did he admire? What was the argument about earlier on the phone?

Out in the garden at home, what with the weather being so fine, Eugenie has crawled through the jungle and hacked her way to Hollywood, wearing Mrs Bliss' Midnight Blemish lipstick. She acts out a screen test for the tree, recalling the film from TV last night. Bang, Bang, you're fucking dead you are. The tree is dead. The garden's overgrown. Mrs Bliss stands motionless on the back steps, the wind tugging her light dress, shagging her light hair. She stands there so long, so still, so passively wild, that Eugenie notices and waves. She is ashamed, she owns up to her, she is noble, she is protective. She would never understand how she felt about Mrs Bliss. Years later, when she grew up, she would remember her like this.

It's hard to tell whether Mrs Bliss sees her daughter waving or not. After some moments she disappears back indoors. Paul is boiling water to kill ants. Mrs Bliss sorts the washing at random, making two heaps of dirty laundry on the kitchen floor.

'Are there ghosts here? I saw a white dog in my bedroom when I woke up,' says Paul, impatient to see some steam from the kettle.

'Ask your father . . .' She bites her lip. It's the first time she's deferred questions to her husband.

No, there are no ghosts. Sometimes there are things that can't be explained. That's very important to remember. Those are the things you must pursue. That's where hope lies.

Mrs Bliss stops sorting socks to look at Paul. He's watching her close with his small intense eyes.

'Let's make a wish,' says Mrs Bliss. 'Let's wish for a visitor, someone rich, with influence.'

'OK,' says Paul, forgetting the boiling water with his interest in the new game.

They both close their eyes and wish. A nano-second passes and the front door bell rings. They open their eyes and stare at each other.

'Answer it,' whispers Mrs Bliss. Paul goes, leaving his mother to contemplate the possibility that she is psychic.

He returns with a smart, small, slim woman in a mini tweed-suit and white boots.

'I'm looking for Mr Bliss.'

'Who are you?' says Eugenie, her lips a bright smear, even in the shadows of the doorway.

The woman smiles. 'I've come about a room.'

'It's taken,' says Mrs Bliss. She doesn't know whether she has summoned this stranger or not, but she wants to get rid of her.

'This is my address and phone number,' says the woman, slipping a small white card on top of the dirty laundry. 'If there are any vacancies in the future, let me know. I like this part of town.' She extends her hand in a departing gesture. Mrs Bliss gets off her knees and nods. The card reads Leila B. King (photographer), America Street, SE1.

'Sorry to have troubled you.' Ms King turns back to the door. Eugenie stands aside and then follows her into the ill-lit hallway.

Yes, thinks Mrs Bliss. I am troubled. But that was yesterday. Today it's the party and I'll fix things. Maybe get drunk and go for a ride in the taxi like we used to. It's all right, people come and go here all the time. I am just a woman of the world, walking up and down in it.

There are no more events that day. Perhaps there's nothing more Mrs Bliss wants to wish for right now.

Late at night. Paul and Eugenie are in bed, talking long after lights-out. British Summertime has plucked them forward into a sweet season of long evenings. Sounds of lots of laughing from downstairs. Drum beats and guitars. Eugenie lies on her bed tapping time.

'Shall we go and look?' says Paul.

'If they're all down there, let's stay up here. We'll go into their room.'

They pad across the landing. The big bedroom has built-in wardrobes either side of an enormous window. The sill accommodates both kids easily. The city lights stretch on forever. Tall buildings wrapped in scaffolding and green plastic, men slicing pavements like they're drilling for oil, cars block roads wide and narrow, music rock-steady-beating through open doors, women shout greetings across shopping arcades, sirens wail, tourists climb on one another's backs and take photos. Eugenie pictures her city that is yet to be explored and lived in. Jumping out of windows, where would she land? In some other garden, sneaking in through the back door to sleep in a new bed? She starts in on her Changeling stories. Paul lets her talk a while and then explains how he's fallen out with his mates Frank and Khalid. Eugenie asks why. Paul says they were laughing at him. Eugenie puts her arm round his shoulder. Same height and weight.

'That's 'cos you're funny.' She studies his spiky face. 'I'll put a spell on you and then you won't be frightened of being alone. I'm not scared. Look at that crowded world out there.'

Above the Beach Boys they hear the sound of banging. Rapid thuds, then silence. Rapid thuds. A hammer. Halfway down the first flight of stairs, Mr and Mrs Bliss are laying a new (secondhand) carpet on top of the old one. Tacks between their teeth, they take it in turns with the hammer. Beyond them in the hallway couples are dancing. Mr and

Mrs Bliss look up to see their identikit son and daughter, bare toes curled round the top step.

'We're fixing things,' says Mr Bliss. 'A little late I know.' They continue nailing the carpet baggily to the turn in the sweeping staircase, then Mr Bliss goes off to make cocoa. The four of them drink together, perched on two steps.

'Happy?' says Mr Bliss. He winks and pulls a funny face. An old habit of his that seems uncharacteristic now.

The kids are drowsy. They take one of them each and put them back to bed. Mrs Bliss closes the door real gentle-like. 'Happy?' she says. Mr Bliss, hands deep in the pocket of his corduroys, asks her almost shyly if she'd like to go for a drive. She agrees, but says she'll change first. Mr Bliss listens at the door of the big bedroom, following her high-heels across the floorboards. Is that the sound of her voice hushed on the phone again?

Mr Bliss goes downstairs and finds Peroxide Joan shimmering in a patch of moonlight by the open french windows. 'You want me to keep an eye on the kids?' she says, pricking him playfully on the chin with a little wooden cocktail stick. 'You're very handsome, but you need looking after.' She's young but she's not naive. She excuses herself and glitzes off in her sequinned Top Shop dress; gets a Raymond Chandler off the book-shelf and goes upstairs to the landing for half an hour or so.

Mr Bliss starts up the black taxi outside. 'The Girl From Impanema' is playing on the radio. He sings along:

> Tall and tanned and young and lovely
> the girl from Ipanema goes walking

and when she passes
each one she passes goes aahh!

Mr Bliss shouts out of tune all the way:

Ooooh! but he watch her so sadly
how can he tell her he loves her
Yes he would give his heart gladly
but it's day when she walks to the sea . . .
she looks straight ahead not at him
Tall and tanned and young and lovely
the girl from Ipanema goes walking
and when she passes
he smiles but she doesn't see
she just doesn't see
no she doesn't see.

It's March 1969. Mr Bliss feels the blood warm in his body with the approaching spring and cheap wine. Who would live at any time other than this? Men walking out there in space, free love, sit-ins, love-ins, technicolor, left-wing politics, french intellectuals, Krushchev, and so on.

They confess to each other every few months. Recently they started using the taxi. It seemed perfect. Sliding back the window that separated the cab from the back, whispering in deserted streets, whispering in traffic jams. He switches the radio off when Mrs Bliss gets in. She's wearing slacks and an Arran sweater, even though it's a warm night. Her hair is pulled back.

'Where to?' says Mr Bliss.

'1965.' She laughs, as if there is an edge of malice under her serenity. 'How much?'

'Five pounds.'

Mr Bliss flicks on the meter and drives off. Around. Takes some of the short cuts he knows she likes. He waits for her to start talking. Mrs Bliss has flipped down the seat behind him. He can smell her soap smell.

'Why 1965?'

Mrs Bliss lights a Senior Service and exhales deeply. '1965 . . . I don't know. Things were good. I loved you ever since that first time I saw you in the lift but I didn't know it then. That was ten years ago.' She looks at the dark pavements rushing by. Mr Bliss checks her in the rear-view mirror from time to time.

'1965. We left for the city, found Macklin Street. Remember, after we bought the house we went there when it was still empty and put Sellotape crosses where we thought our things should go, and we screwed in the big bedroom and afterwards put a cross on the floor for the bed. And then after we moved in . . . and none of the things ended up where the marks had been, and since then I feel as if . . . as if I'm always dragging furniture about trying to fix things right, but it won't save me . . .'

Mrs Bliss looks at the meter. Three pounds.

'1965. Since then I've learned some things. I know you're a taxi driver, you have lots of women you drive places, you meet interesting people. You dream of being a filmmaker and making Marxist films. You prefer plain shirts. Your father drowned. You like wine, not beer. You weigh eleven stones, five pounds. You fall in love easily. You are afraid of disease. You rarely buy clothes for yourself. You like Woolworth's. You went to La Finca when you found out I'd been unfaithful and got off your face. You seek self-confidence and mistrust fragility. You like women better than men. You are afraid to turn the TV off if you leave the room. And . . . I know who Marian is –'

Mrs Bliss pauses in devil-may-care drunkenness. The ash falls off the end of her cigarette on to the cab floor. The meter reads four pounds. They stop at a red light for the first time. Mrs Bliss fumbles for a wish. What can she wish for now? That she didn't know these things? That he would hit the gas and speed them back or forwards in time? For riches? For Marian's exile? For a one-way ticket to Los Angeles? First prize in a beauty contest? For the innocence of Paul and Eugenie? For immortality?

'I wish I didn't know these things,' she says as the meter hits five pounds, 'and I want my old name back. I can't live in these times.'

Mr Bliss pulls over to the kerb, gets out and joins his wife on the back seat. 'Will you drive me for a while?'

She nods. 'Where to?'

'Here and now, just around.'

'How much?'

'A quid.'

'Is that all?'

'I want to get back to the party.'

They swap places. Mrs Bliss re-sets the meter and skids off. She knows she's steering the boat now. Sweet Saints how she likes speed. It's the end of a decade, or fucking ought to be. Mr Bliss shouts his confession in three sentances: 'I like it here! I am in love! I am torn apart!' and then shuts up. Mrs Bliss drives round and round the block till one pound is clocked up. Not long. Then screeches a U-turn and cruises back home.

Eugenie, kneeling on her bed, sees the black cab pull up outside. She sees her father get out and walk to the front, open the door real gentle-like, and offer his hand to her mother. She thinks she sees them smile as they dip under the overgrown hedge. Then they're lost from view.

The Lady in the Desert

·

SYLVIA BROWNRIGG

I've heard about these starvation diets you can go on; I thought it sounded like a good idea. So I decided to move to the desert. No temptations, right? Just sand and sky, the occasional constellation after dark. Sounds relaxing.

I'm trying to lose ten pounds.

Everyone says it should be pretty easy. I mean, I'm not like Abigail, who really could afford to drop thirty or even forty before she'd feel comfortable tanning on the beach. Abigail shops at the Lady Bountiful store where they sell the bigger items. Says the saleswomen there are so friendly and nice. Don't make you feel awkward, tell you you look good. Hold your other-coloured options while you pace back and forth in front of the mirror. Walking the walk, giving a twirl.

Then there's Barb. She's never looked the same since her kids. Never lost that weight back. Still has great wads of dough on either hip, 'love-handles' you can call them for a joke, or if anyone you love actually handles them – doesn't happen in my life, not any more, not since Tony – but we all know what they really are is fat, fat, fat.

I'd like to be thin, myself. Obviously I haven't got a big problem with my weight – I'm only trying to lose ten pounds – but I'd like to be just that bit thinner, that people would take a look at me and say to themselves, 'Now how does she keep her shape like that?'

'Serenity,' would be my answer. That and maybe cutting out doughnuts completely and sticking strictly to skimmed milk and margarine. Otherwise it's a state of mind. *Serenity*. I'll smile when I say it. Serene-like. Confident.

That's after I get back from the desert. While I'm here I don't have to worry about ordinary day-to-day things, like what per cent fat in the milk or yogurt, because of course here there isn't anything like that at all. No refrigerators. No dairy. No health and international aisle, no frozen veg, no party and picnicware, no clingwrap.

Nothing, like I said, but sand and sky.

I took a walk my first day here. It would be easy to get lost, I knew, so I took a multipack of sugarless gum I'd brought with me and left the wrappers sticking up in the sand for signposts. They stood up like bright little flags from around the world, showing up to mark my path. I chewed a lot of sugarless before I realised I could use the wrappers without actually opening up and chewing all the gum inside. I'm so stupid sometimes! And it makes sense to save some gum for later. What else am I going to have to distract me round about Day Seven of my diet?

It was a pleasant walk, though. Smooth and yellow-white, a dry smell in the air. I wouldn't have minded a little bird-song, maybe a tree or a building on the horizon to break it up a little, but otherwise it was enjoyable. A thin breeze whisked around my face every now and then, which was refreshing, what with the heat here. I wore my sun visor for protection and a dab of sunblock on my nose – I hate that Rudolph effect when you forget.

The sand got in my tennis shoes and made it hard to walk, but I got my rhythm going after a while. It's like being on a ship. On our honeymoon we went on a cruise ship and it took me some time to get my 'sea legs.' (I'll never forget it – sliding back and forth along the deck, holding on to Tony, both of us laughing. He wasn't any better at it than me; in fact he was the one who couldn't keep his food down, poor guy.) Here, I guess, you could say it took me a few minutes to get my 'sand legs,' but I did develop the technique after a while. You've got to relax, let your foot go all loose and follow the shape of the sand dune. Be flexible. Just don't expect solid ground and you're fine.

That's the last time I'm going to mention our honeymoon.

So I walked along, planting my gum wrappers every so often, humming a tune from *South Pacific*, one of my favourites. I thought about Jean's daughter's wedding in a couple of weeks and wondered if she's really going to look okay in that dress. They've had quite a to-do about that dress, with Jean telling her – and I agreed – that the *one* thing a wedding dress has to be is long. And with her legs! But Nickie insists she's going to wear it. 'It's the in thing, Mom,' she said, which you can't argue with, apparently. I'll be curious to see the pictures. Jean hugging her daughter, trying to smile like it isn't killing her.

I also thought a little, on my walk, about whether I really feel like paying more taxes like they're always talking about. I say, show me some results! Where does the money go? I mean, what are we paying for exactly, besides people's private jets and ski vacations, and is that what the government is all about? This somehow got me worrying about the situation in the Middle East. All this sand, I was bound to start thinking about it. Why can't people get along there, is what I never understand. What is their problem, and is it worth it to keep fighting about it? They say Armageddon's lurking there, though I don't know that I believe them. Made me hotter just to think about it.

In this way the time passed fast, and when I'd worked up a good sweat I decided to head back. They say it's good to get some kind of aerobic exercise for your heart every day, if possible. This walk definitely qualified. I was a little dizzy by the end but I think that had more to do with the sun and some of those uncomfortable thoughts than because I'd over-strained myself. I'm basically in good shape. I only get out of breath by the third floor, where I work.

Luckily I was smart enough to bring an umbrella with me on this trip, so when I got back to home-base I opened it up, propped it in the sand and stretched out under it. The sun was slipping in the sky, it was late afternoon. I was doing great so far: what with the walk and my thoughts and making sure I could follow the gum wrappers back, I hadn't thought about food more than a couple of times. Anyway, it was too hot to have much of an appetite.

I'll tell you the truth, though. What I did have a big craving for there, under the umbrella, in that late heat, was a milkshake. A milkshake would have gone down so perfect then: a nice, creamy chocolate shake with a rich malty aftertaste. A McDonald's milkshake, in fact. They make pretty good ones, you might not realise it but it's true. It's the malt I love.

If not that, I could have gone for a fruit smoothie, my second choice. To be healthy. The kind brightly coloured Hawaiian-type girls sell in stands on the street to make you feel virtuous. Strawberries, bananas, honey, coconut, ice and milk – it can't be a whole lot less calories than a milkshake, but I guess at least you get the fibre and the vitamins.

I had to settle for a swig from my canteen. What could I do? It was a starvation diet. Rules are rules. Besides, there wasn't anything else available.

To make myself stop thinking about the milkshake I took a novel out of my bag. My mouth was full of these juices – juices of the hunger for strawberries, the hunger for that malt flavour, for the periodic crunch of the ice between your teeth that makes you shiver.

I lay down under the umbrella using the canteen for a pillow. I tried to focus on my book. It was about an airport. Something was happening in an airport, someone caught sight of someone else who was supposed to be on a different flight but instead was on a flight to one of those cities that always shows up in books like that, Dubai maybe, or Nicosia. It was a thriller.

I read three pages before I fell into a thick, hot doze. I dreamt about Daquiris. Kind of like a party we had on the ship that time, though that was years ago. Rum, ice, crushed fruit: the feeling that none of it would end. They do that to you, vacations. Make you forget what's real.

When I woke up, I couldn't even remember the names of any of the characters in the book, and I knew I'd have to read those first few pages again.

It didn't take me long to develop a routine. I find a routine makes the day manageable. Otherwise you're sliding all over the place, wondering where to go. That's why I, unlike a lot of people I know, am pretty happy about my job. In fact I was really beginning to miss some of the girls already and to wonder what they were getting up to. Abigail, Barb, Jean. Even Ellen. Even *Nancy*.

I'm not saying I didn't need a vacation. People said it was time I took one, that I was looking tired. Looking like I'd been under a lot of stress, which I had. The things you go through after a loss, you know? I'll tell you what, though. I didn't tell anyone where I was going, or about the diet. The worst thing is when you tell people something like that and then break it. Everyone knows. The second you leave the room they say, 'I knew she'd never be able to stick with it. I've seen how much she enjoys her french fries.' This way, when I go back, there will just be the shock; the silence; the admiration. 'What happened to *you*?' they'll say. A little jealous, of course. A little disappointed. 'You look *terrific*!'

So this is how my routine goes. I don't have a watch, which makes it tricky, but I go by the temperature and how high the sun is, white-hot, in the colourless sky.

DAWN: Wake up. Stretch. Do half an hour (approx.) of calisthenics.

MORNING BREAK: Gargle once with water, then spit. Generous helping of water that's kept pretty cool by the desert night. Take one mega-vitamin. (Hopefully that's not cheating.)

MORNING: Dress. Take a sand bath. A little itchy at first, but I've gotten used to them. Tidy clothes, roll up sleeping bag; it's good to stay disciplined. Spend a couple of hours on organisational matters – writing up next year's Christmas list, for example, or planning for my summer budget.

LUNCH: Three sips *maximum* of diet cola. It's the one thing I allowed myself to bring. But I only brought one can because I felt guilty about it, so I have to ration the supply.

HIGH NOON: When the ball of heat is directly overhead. Nap. Sometimes it takes me a minute, because the diet cola has jazzed me up (I should have gotten caffeine-free), but then the heat soaks through to me. I find the rest useful.

EARLY AFTERNOON: Go for a walk. I've got the gum wrapper system down to perfection. Sing a couple of songs from *South Pacific* or *Guys and Dolls*, or occasionally *Oklahoma!* There are three walks I do: the one where you go over the gentle slope into the slightly cooler dip of grey sand; the straightforward, straight-ahead walk where nothing much changes; and the one where I walk in the other direction completely, where eventually you see the faint outline of a clump of trees. An oasis. I call this one Mirage Mile, because I don't believe those trees really exist.

AFTERNOON: Temperature's a tad cooler. I read under the umbrella. I try to keep my attention on the thriller – that first guy is dead by now, I know that much – but I still keep losing the thread and forgetting the characters' names, so I often have to go back to re-read. Every now and then a thought of a turkey club, or even a salad bar salad with ranch-style dressing, wings across my mind and temporarily blots out the novel. And then there are thoughts of Tony, though I try to wipe those out before they even get there.

EVENING: The sun is low in the sky. I'm beat. It's been a long day. Dinner is a slice of sugarless gum. The good thing about the multipack is it has different flavours. Sometimes just for fun I'll ask myself, 'So what'll it be tonight?' And I'll answer, lifting up my sunglasses as if to take a closer look at the menu, 'I think I'll have the strawberry.'

Dessert is water.

Last, but not least – my nightcap. One brief shot of whisky. Again, maybe a stretching of the rules – but so worth it. It calms and relaxes me after everything I've done. Besides, the pounds are melting off me, I can tell. I don't have a scale, but you know how it is, you can just tell. Your heart feels lighter. Your ankles that bit more delicate.

The only problem with the nightcap, on a bad night, is it can make you a little melancholy. The kinds of things that creep up on you: people you miss; things you wish you'd done; age; and the fact that another baseball season is already almost upon us.

NIGHT: Ink-blue and cold. I'm feeling pretty sleepy by now. I change into my nightgown and settle down in my comfy sleeping bag. Say a quick prayer, maybe. Think about my friends at home, wonder how they're doing. Count the days till Jean's daughter's wedding and hope they haven't been fighting too much. Finally, just before sleep, my last delicious indulgence of the day. I think about the chocolate cake I'll have when I make it out of here. Thick fudge-creamy icing. Coconut. Moist, deep brown, sweet. Smelling like paradise. Like the cake in that restaurant the night I first met Tony.

I've decided to extend the diet, and the trip. It's just going so well. I'm sure they'll understand at work. It's too bad I can't call them to tell them – there's no phone here, of course. They'll just have to manage without me.

The girls won't recognise me when I'm back. 'How'd you *do* it?' they'll ask, astonished. 'What's your secret?' I won't let on how I did it. I'll smile mysteriously. I'll treat myself to one or two new outfits, and watch people noticing me with a whole different attitude.

I've been talking to Tony some about it at night – about how great it feels to be this much lighter. I think he's proud of me. Don't worry, I'm not going crazy! I know Tony's gone and everything. I'm not that confused. Still, I find it a comfort to have a little chat with him before I go to sleep. Jean's daughter's wedding has come and gone, so I don't have that to think about any more. I gave up on the novel. One of the guys died by being thrown in a swimming pool bound and gagged, before he had a chance to tell the other guy, the airport guy, where he'd stashed the document that exposed the true nature of the business. I lost interest at that point. Besides, who needs references to swimming pools? I live in the desert now, and have to get used to it.

Tony always was a quiet guy. It's not so hard to get used

to him not talking back. Frankly I just find it a help having him here at all, keeping me company, spurring me on with his silent ways, boosting my confidence about how terrific I'm looking. 'Thin, huh?' I'll say to Tony in the afternoon, after I get back from my walk. The sky will sometimes seem to darken and I may nearly fall over. When I get my balance again I'm even more excited. 'It's hard to tell I'm the same person, isn't it?' I'll say, and he can't do anything but agree.

I have a great ambition for the end of the day today. It's something I always meant to do before I go. I'm going to take my day's walk today on Mirage Mile, and see, though I know by definition it's impossible, if I can make it all the way to the trees at the end.

Tony's agreed to come with me. He thinks it's a nutty plan, but finally he had to go along with it. It was that way with our honeymoon, too. He thought a cruise trip sounded awful – to tell you the truth, Tony always hated the water, which makes it such a terrible coincidence that he died how he did – but when he saw that I had my heart set on it, what could he do? Tony was always sweet to me that way. I told him about the pictures I'd seen of a jewel-blue sea being cut in half by a diamond-white ship, on which all the people were blonde and thin and smiling. Tony said, 'We're not blonde or thin but I guess we could smile,' and so he booked us the tickets. I want to tell him now – Hey, Tony, at least *I* am now, you know! At least *I'm* thin now! And who knows what they do to you in heaven, maybe he is too.

So he's agreed to come along. I explained to him my marker system. I explained how you put the little wrappers in the ground like they were the flags of the United Nations, as if this walk we would take might somehow ensure world peace. I didn't tell him about higher taxes or the question of Armageddon. I thought it would depress him. Besides, I don't think about that stuff so much myself any more. When you're happy with yourself, the way I am now I'm thin, you don't have to focus on other people's ills.

My mind's so clear now. I've long since finished the diet cola, so I don't have that around to pollute me. I abandoned the exercise regime, it seemed a waste of time. I've forgotten exactly what the work I had to do on my desk before I left was – which I figure by now someone else has picked up anyway. I think about Jean, and Abigail and Barb, but in my mind now they are blurred and yellow, wearing the weak smiles of the somewhat forlorn. Be *happy*, I wish I could tell them from across this great expanse of desert. Shed that weight! Feel good about yourself! When you do, little things like wedding dresses won't get to you at all! If I can reach this kind of contentment, girls, I'm sure that *you* can.

'Happy talkie talk and happy talk . . .' I prepare for my walk, singing from *South Pacific*. When Tony's not watching me, I allow myself to gaze out at the sheer bone-whiteness of the sand and imagine what I'll find if I reach the oasis. Great tall palm trees dripping sweet dates. A coconut spilling its creamy smooth milk. An orange grove, possibly, studded with that sweetest, purest fruit that hot countries provide. And by the deep-blue pond of the clear cool water, Tony dangling his toes, sunning himself in his grey trunks, enjoying life, his baseball cap jutting out over his eyes. This time there will be no accident. This time we won't lose him to his heart's water-logged failure. I look at him longingly in the oasis and walk towards him, my now tanned lean arms outstretched, my thin body model-glamorous and graceful. I take an armful of the fruits around me and approach him, my dear Tony, the man I've loved since that first chocolate cake.

He smiles at me but also tilts his head like something is bugging him.

'Ah, ah, ah –' he says to me in a scolding voice. 'Rules are rules, hon!'

He winks at me as if to indulge me, then relieves my arms of all that fruit. He takes an orange and slowly starts to peel it, watching me watch him as the peels spiral to the ground.

I want to kiss him, the orange on his lips looks so good. But Tony's a mirage, and I know if I kiss him he'll melt away. So I let him get on with eating his orange. I have to be happy to keep my distance. I sit over on the other side of the big blue pond, and wait for myself weightlessly, hushed, to evanesce.

Pale Cecilia and the Policewoman

.

MARION URCH

Cecilia stood in her father's bedroom. her eyes scanning the dark mahogany wardrobes that dominated the room. She traced the outline of each of the doors, seeking some irregularity: a door left slightly ajar perhaps, or the sleeve of a shirt caught in mid-flight between the door and its frame. She was looking for a sign, a small touch of intimacy, a hint, a gesture of invitation. But each of the doors was resolutely closed, neat and rigid as officers on parade.

Standing within the shadows, Cecilia looked faint and lacking in substance, her silhouette projected into the gloom by the watery light that struggled through the heavy net of the curtains. Access to her father's bedroom had ended at the same time as her childhood. Since then she'd peeped regularly around the door when no one was in the house, as if she might catch a glimpse of something in the empty room. Now the wardrobes loomed up around her on all sides. From floor to ceiling, three walls of the room were entirely covered by the heavy panelled doors. In the modest pre-war council house the room tucked away at the back was almost a sanctified place.

Cecilia opened the central mahogany door to reveal the shiny silver jewel hidden within the murky interior. As a child she had often wondered what the mirror reflected on when it was shut away in the darkness. She knew that the mirror stayed bright and opened other doors. Like her eyelids, when she closed them, showed her other images – her mind's repertoire of scenes and pictures she played back again and again and never tired of. She stood obediently in the middle of the room and looked at what the mirror showed her. Pale and white and naked, she stood with her hair loose down her back and her hands neatly folded in front of her. She felt very calm. Breathing deeply from the pit of her stomach she felt her hands rise, exhaling she watched her breath steam the mirror. In the gloomy half light her pale skin glowed like a luminous statue. With each deep breath she felt more tranquil and more alive, as if she was truly breathing for the first time. She practised a faint smile in the mirror and watched it linger as it became real. She knew she need never be nervous again. She need never scurry and jump. She knew that the old feeling that she was always wrong was falling away from her with every breath she took. No more twitching and peeping around doors. All those feelings were gone as certainly as They were gone.

She was as sure that her parents were gone as she was of the bones in her body that seemed to be hardening and strengthening as she stood there. She wasn't sure whether it was her fault they were gone and she didn't care. Maybe she had done something. Maybe the images that came to her when she closed her eyes had driven them away. She didn't care anyway, because now she could do as she liked, and so she stood in the forbidden heart of the house, as calm in her nakedness as a Madonna in her blue robes. She looked hard into the mirror, watching herself and waiting for a transformation. Her body looked soft and boneless, a fleshy liquid form. She looked white as a grub, the white folds of her belly marked by fine violet lines. She was too smooth. Without muscles and untouched by the sun, she was almost blue. The long hair, which was loose now and brushed the top of her buttocks, was the same pale putty colour as the hair under her arms and between her legs. Her nipples and her mouth were a pale shrimpy inverted pink rather than a colour in full bloom. Cecilia looked and looked. She was thirty-nine years old yet she looked newly born, as if she'd just emerged from the cracks of an egg.

She swung her hair out of curiosity. Her long straight hair without a kink or a curl in it, which her mother had always bound into a tight plait every night. Her hair which hadn't been cut since her sister had died. Cecilia didn't mind that her hair was so long and always plaited, because she didn't feel it belonged to her any more than her body did. She'd always felt that she belonged to her parents and she'd been grateful to them. And she was alive, wasn't she, and without Breda she was all they had. So now she stood naked in front of the mirror and swung her hair and examined herself as thoroughly as if she were a brand new doll. For the first time, Cecilia was beginning to feel that her body was her own.

After she'd called at the Bryants, Mrs Dawson had marched directly to the police station.

'I always go around on Thursdays. To collect the St Vincent de Paul envelopes. For the parish. The Bryants and I are in the Queen of Heaven. Edna, Mrs Bryant that is, is always waiting for me by the back door. It's been the same for I don't know how long, fifteen years, sixteen. But yesterday I got there and there was no sign of anybody and no tea waiting. And then, doesn't their Cecilia come sailing in from the hall, with nothing on her except a slip of a dressing gown. She wouldn't be walking around like that if Edna was in the house.'

Mrs Dawson paused and the officer began to speak. 'And what exactly is the nature of your complaint? A young girl in her dressing gown? The lack of a cup of tea? A change of routine, perhaps?'

'I tell you, something's happened. She's always there on Thursdays, always.'

The officer filed an 'alleged' report of two missing persons. 'Don't you worry, lovey. I'll send an officer around there in a couple of days. Alright?'

WPC Donaghue walked heavily towards number thirty-two, Acacia Road. It was Monday afternoon and the day was dragging slowly towards a close. She had only been out of police training for a couple of weeks, but still she was livid at the way they'd just treated her at the station. They were keeping her away from heavy police work and she knew they'd given her the old lady's complaint because they didn't take either her or the old lady seriously.

WPC Donaghue was a policewoman because her family had always been in the police force. Where some families have a run of priests or nuns, the Donaghues had policemen. It had become a matter of defiance with them. While Ireland had struggled for independence, the Donaghues had remained in the Royal Constabulary, despite pressure from their neighbours. Now they were policemen in England and Anne was the latest one to carry the torch of Donaghue stubbornness.

'They'll never make a policewoman out of that big, useless lump of a girl,' her father had said.

'Just like her father,' said her mother.

'Why shouldn't I join the police force?' she'd asked. 'I'm a Donaghue as much as I'm a girl, aren't I?'

And so she became a policewoman because of the principle of the thing and because stubbornness, 'principles' and a sense of tradition were valued in the force. She was also a policewoman because it suited her way of thinking. Evidence and circumstance, proof and alibis. She liked things in their place. As she walked down the quiet suburban streets she smoothed down her jacket proudly. The uniform streamlined her ample shape into a solid formidable form. She liked that. Her breasts were smoothed and flattened and the rigid front of the jacket protected the soft underbelly that curved beneath it. But encased within the sharp lines of the heavy navy suit, her body was beginning to protest. It was becoming a sticky evening at the end of a long humid day. She pulled at the jacket of her suit and resisted the urge to scratch. Beneath her pristine exterior her body swelled and sweated and itched.

In the damp meadows beyond Acacia Road ghost moths, unchanged for two-hundred million years, flew just before dusk. After fertilisation the straw-coloured females, with their brick-red markings, dropped their eggs freely on the grass as they flew. White when laid, their new eggs soon turned to black.

WPC Donaghue walked straight around to the back door of number thirty-two. A flap of net curtain from the window waved at her through the open door and she hesitated for only a moment before peering around it. The kitchen was neat and orderly, except for wind-blown curtains billowing from open windows. She stepped inside and, calling into the emptiness of the house, she heard footsteps padding down the stairs. While she was waiting for their owner to appear she glanced around again. On the kitchen table there was a tray with a tin of biscuits and two mugs on it. In the bottom of each mug there appeared to be a mixture of sugar and cocoa. Next to the mugs lay a teaspoon and a saucer with four biscuits on it. The biscuits looked soft, as if they had been exposed to the air too long. Over on the stove a small saucepan was half filled with milk.

When the footsteps reached the kitchen door, WPC Donaghue turned. Her eyes flicked quickly over the loose hair, the tattered kimono and the bare feet.

'Miss Bryant?' she asked. From the description at the

station she had been expecting a prim and dusty spinster still living at home at thirty-nine.

'Miss Bryant,' she said again. 'I wonder if you'd mind answering a few questions. It's about your parents.'

A nervous smile rippled across Cecilia's lips as she hovered by the kitchen door. 'They haven't come back yet,' she said, as if the policewoman should really be speaking to them.

'No, that's why I'm here. Do you mind if I sit down?'

WPC Donaghue pulled out her notebook as she settled into a chair. She still felt slightly unnerved by the hovering Cecilia and the heavy navy serge of her skirt prickled the backs of her thighs. She cleared her throat before she spoke.

'When did you last see your parents, Miss Bryant?'

'Gone,' said Cecilia, like a forlorn child. Then she giggled, straightened up abruptly, and said, 'They didn't come back. They went for a walk and they didn't come back. I don't think they'll ever come back – do you?'

WPC Donaghue repeated her question. Cecilia cradled her elbows and rocked herself from side to side. She smiled, enjoying the feel of her hair swinging behind her.

'When did I last see them?' she puzzled. 'Yesterday? The day before yesterday?' Cecilia shrugged and her eyes glazed over.

'Miss Bryant,' the policewoman snapped. 'It's Monday today, your neighbours say they haven't seen Mr and Mrs Bryant for a number of days now. There are six pints of milk on the doorstep. Mrs Dawson called on Thursday and said no one was in. Except you, of course. Does that jog your memory?'

Cecilia stopped rocking and stared. 'Would you like a cup of tea?' she said. Sitting down opposite the police-woman she mused aloud.

'Mrs Dawson. Yes, Mrs Dawson came, but it was too late. I didn't know where the envelope was. That was Thursday was it? It was before then. Maybe the day before. They went for a walk but they didn't come back.'

'Wednesday,' said WPC Donaghue. 'You think they disappeared on Wednesday?'

'Disappeared?' repeated Cecilia. 'Have they disappeared? They didn't come back.'

The policewoman took a deep breath and said, 'What time on Wednesday?'

Cecilia smiled sympathetically. 'I'm sorry, officer, I don't know.'

WPC Donaghue pointed at the supper things on the table. 'Are they from Wednesday?'

'I suppose they must be. I don't like cocoa and I'm always in bed by the time they have theirs.'

'And what time is that?'

'They go for a walk. Then they come home, then they have cocoa. Then they go to bed,' Cecilia said, in a bored sing-song voice. 'Will you come and visit me again? We don't get many visitors.'

'So they go for a walk in the evenings?'

'Mmm.' Cecilia sighed again and WPC Donaghue finally gave up and heaved herself from her seat. She left Cecilia at the table, wrapping her hair absent-mindedly around her throat.

*

Walking away from the house, the policewoman shuddered as if traces of Cecilia still clung in the air like cobwebs around her. 'It shouldn't be allowed,' she thought, but she felt protective towards her too, as if she were a child again and Cecilia her doll. Buttoning up her little dress right to the top and folding the layers of her skirt down around her legs. 'Baby doll. My baby doll.' WPC Donaghue pulled herself up short. What on earth was she thinking of? 'Ah, well, it was late, wasn't it. There's no crime there, not yet anyway,' she thought as she watched the lights of the living rooms pop shut around her.

A week passed by and Mrs Dawson called at the police station to complain that nothing had been done.

'There was always something wrong with that girl. You ought to look into it. Left the milk out for over a week she did, and in this weather too,' she said before she marched righteously out of the station.

In the garden of thirty-two, Acacia Road, Longhorn moths whirled about in the clearings and among the shrubs, the metallic sheen of their hind wings glittering brightly in the sunlight.

As the hours trickled into days and the days formed slowly into a week, Cecilia gradually laid claim to each of the rooms in the house. The first thing she'd done was discard her clothes, those sensible, arid garments that she and her mother had chosen together over the years. In the small box-room that had served her as a bedroom, she'd emerged naked, like a born-again Ophelia, from the mass of dun-coloured clothes that swirled around her ankles. Clothing in every shade of brown – beige, mushroom, earth, rust – lay piled up around her single unmade bed as if it were a re-opened grave.

She went silently from room to room, moving objects out of place, leaving doors ajar, unhooking safety catches, opening drawers; until she remembered the old cardboard box buried in the back of her father's wardrobe.

Once upon a time, a long time ago, before her father had used old furniture to build the wardrobes in his room, before Breda had died, before even Cecilia was born, life at Acacia Road had been different. Number thirty-two had been filled with dreams. Foolish dreams, her Mother called them later. Foolish dreams and faded laughter. But once Edna had smiled and they'd danced around the sitting room. There was proof too – Mr Bryant had made sure of that – folded neatly away and layered with tissue; the evidence was in the cardboard box.

Before Breda had died Mr Bryant used to tell them stories of his travels across the seas. India, America, China. All over the world, across every sea; he had been everywhere they could think of. And for every place he went he brought back proof. Gifts from a sailor to his beautiful young wife. And the young wife had smiled and they'd waltzed around the room.

But the young wife became weary. 'What's the use of silks and satins and jewels when there's beds to make and children to feed?' So the collection of presents was bundled up and flung into the gloom of the mahogany wardrobes, until those quiet Saturdays when Edna was out of the house. Then Mr Bryant laid out his treasures on the floor around him, as if he was a bazaar owner and these were his exotic wares, regaling Breda and Cecilia with the story of each item; the strange place it had come from and the exotic name attached. Each time he recited the stories in exactly the same way, his eyes glazed over and smiling; such hopes he'd had, such high hopes.

Until Breda died. Then the box went back into the cupboard, the mahogany door was firmly shut and the door of her father's room stayed permanently closed. Until now.

Now Cecilia opened all the doors and left them open. And left all the lights on too. No more going from room to room, flicking light switches and herself, into and out of darkness. She'd flung open the doors and switched on the lights, brutally she thought; as if the house was an ageing woman who hid from the light, her illusions of youth now in tatters and her faded shabbiness exposed. And she'd opened the central door of the mahogany wardrobes as if the mirror was her heart. She felt her pulse jump as she watched the blood pumping in a vein of her neck.

The cupboard with the cardboard box was so laden with mothballs that she'd felt almost drunk from the assault of camphor and formalin as she'd opened the door. The exact words her father had used came back to Cecilia as she pulled out the box. The kimono lay across the top: 'Hong Kong, 1947. At night the streets shone from a hundred neon reflections. Beautiful oriental whores, perfect as dolls, sashayed down the streets, picking their way through the sewers. The fat tails of rats flying as they scurried through the garbage.' She smiled, remembering the words as she held up the kimono. The heavy black satin had dulled to brown in places and frayed away in others. The golden dragon had breathed fire in front of a vivid blossom tree. Land without shadows. She could imagine it. The fire had faded to the colour of congealed blood and the golden threads of the dragon had broken away in places. It didn't matter. The dragon was sinewy and bold and when she put the kimono on she felt it on her back, hotly, like a new tattoo. She stood up with her arms out and felt the air through the heavy rectangular sleeves that hung like wings at her side. She smiled. After that she wandered the house in the dark kimono with the unravelling golden dragon adorning her back.

From under the kimono and amidst the American cotton, the Mexican silver, and the Chinese silks, she pulled out a heavy tray with silver handles: '1948, Rio de Janeiro.' She imagined that Carnival looked like swarms of butterflies because of that tray. But now the whirling patterns of iridescent pink and lemon and vivid blue were turning to fine powder and dust; the stripped-away wings of hundreds of butterflies lay fading beneath the glass. In places the colour had gone, leaving the frail translucent tracery of wings like skeletal forms or Honesty in winter. But Cecilia didn't notice the damage, she only saw the Carnival swirling behind the glass.

In the front parlour, amidst the dark wood, Cecilia sat with the tray in her lap remembering her father's stories. Night was falling rapidly outside and a moth battered itself against the window, desperate for the light. A Death-watch beetle was tapping its way to the surface of the heavy oak sideboard. The natural world was moving faster than her quiet world within the house. In the garden a pale Cinnamon Plume moth, with feathery wings, hovered an invitation. Her caterpillars were feeding on the buds and unripe ovaries of Birdseye Speedwells. All around, pale eggs developed reddish markings while others turned violet or brown. Inside an egg the head of a caterpillar pushed against the thin, translucent shell. In the vegetable patch, the Large White was making lace from cabbage leaves while her caterpillars stripped plants bare, leaving stalks. Inside a curled-up leaf a chrysalis waited within her sulphureous cocoon. Eggs were being fertilised, and hatched, while Cecilia sat and dreamed. The dead things beneath the glass shattered. In a corner of the window a caterpillar was spinning its sticky cocoon while another shed its skin. As Cecilia turned her head, the ship in a bottle on the mantelpiece lost its tiny top sail; the weevils had been working, brought in with the hot-house flowers and the failing vine.

At the police station, the Chief Inspector had finally got around to checking the Bryant case. He scoffed at the idea of it being a case at all, but still, there it was on paper and it had to be dealt with. Donaghue's girl had probably barged in there as if it was a murder case; notebook under her nose and full of theories. And the whole clan of Donaghues like a cardboard halo behind her to back her up, as if that made her any more of a policewoman. The Chief Inspector shouted for WPC Donaghue and pulled out the file. By the time she appeared he'd opened the neatly labelled folder only to find two blank sheets of paper staring up at him. The Chief Inspector looked up and roared. WPC Donaghue opened her mouth and stammered as a hot wave broke over her and ripples of redness moved steadily up her face.

'I've got the notes, sir.'

The Chief Inspector roared again.

'No, sir. I didn't get a statement. Miss Bryant seemed a bit fragile, sir. No sir, I haven't written the notes up, sir. Checked the house? Immediately, sir. Signs of packing? Anything missing? No sir. I'll do that sir. Yes, right away, sir.'

WPC Donaghue was still frantically nodding her head as she grabbed her notebook and ran from the building.

At the Bryant house she was obviously expected. The unused supper things had been replaced by a newly pressed tablecloth with green and orange embroidery. A matching teapot, milk jug and sugar bowl stood on a heavy tray with silver handles. The kettle was boiling on the stove. Cecilia had looked forward to the policewoman's visit, though she knew it wouldn't be too soon; she knew that even the disappearance of her parents didn't make her interesting.

WPC Donaghue sat down heavily, as if the deliberateness of her movements might make her feel more official.

'There's not much we can do in a case like this. We've put them on our missing persons' register but when there's no reason to suspect foul play, well, there's really very little we can do.'

'That's very kind of you officer. You will have a cup of tea?'

'Umm, yes, thank you. There are a few formalities, of course. We should check the house and take a proper statement. Is there anything missing?'

Cecilia poured out two cups of tea and, sitting down opposite WPC Donaghue, she began to speak in a soft low voice.

'It's been more than a week now, and there's still no sign of them, and no news either. Why would they do this, officer? Oh, I know sometimes I imagined a life without them, but I never thought it would happen.'

Cecilia continued to speak in a low even tone that was as persistent as a lullaby, so that WPC Donaghue found herself listening to the sound of the words rather than what she was actually saying.

'Only I've been here for more than a week, officer, and you get to thinking. Well, maybe it is my fault. Oh, I wanted them gone, officer. Sometimes. You can't imagine how it's been. First they wouldn't let me go out and meet anyone, never, since I was a child. And then, too late, they shouted at me that I should go out. Taunting me, taunting me. You should stay in, who'd have you? I don't know, but sometimes I had these feelings. So strong, they were almost real. But it's so easy to get confused, isn't it?' Cecilia spoke like a person who'd never been listened to but continues to speak anyway, out of some compulsion maybe, or from a small hope that someone might catch a word or two.

WPC Donaghue brought herself sharply to attention. 'Your fault?' she repeated.

'Yes, maybe it is my fault. And never anybody in the house, except them, and him so quiet and her taunting. Until the end. It's been like a dead place. And I wanted to go out. She was half pushing me out of the door. "Under my feet, get out from under my feet." But it was too late. I was too afraid. I imagined things. The wardrobes and the coats. I wanted them dead.'

WPC Donaghue jumped in her seat and stared at Cecilia.

'Well, yes, officer, maybe it *was* my fault. Maybe you're right.'

Her voice had become a whisper. 'I wanted them gone. Gone. And I imagined how to do it. But I meant them no harm. Maybe I didn't imagine it at all.'

Cecilia clutched the officer's arm. 'It's not my fault is it, officer? The pickles and the jars. Smaller and smaller. It's not my fault is it?'

WPC Donaghue shivered and shook Cecilia's hand away. She could feel Cecilia's eyes pleading with her as she jumped up from the table and began to search the rooms. In the father's bedroom a swarm of moths flew out when she opened one of the wardrobe doors, so she left the others. As she walked from room to room with Cecilia whispering behind her, she felt as if Cecilia was binding her to her by sticky invisible threads until she couldn't breathe. She left the house very abruptly, taking great gulps of air as she strode off down the road.

Goat moth caterpillars were burrowing into the trees lining Acacia Road and the smell of wood vinegar wafted across WPC Donaghue's path. Fragments of what Cecilia had said came flying back at her as she marched on faster down the road. Oblivious to the sawdust falling from the openings in the trees, she found herself repeating Cecilia's phrase, 'It's not my fault, is it?'

Inside the trees, caterpillars were spinning cocoons from sawdust and silken fibres. She recalled Cecilia's words out loud: 'I wanted them dead, officer.'

'This is silly, just because . . . It doesn't mean . . .' It didn't bear thinking about. She wasn't capable. The girl could hardly dress herself, for God's sake.

As WPC Donaghue walked towards the station she was overwhelmed by an urge to undo her jacket and unbutton the top of her skirt. 'Must have put on a bit of weight,' she thought as she became aware of the band of her skirt and the top of her tights cutting into her waist. Her bra straps and the line of her knickers were slicing into her, pushing her flesh out into soft pads on either side of the tight elastic bands. When she opened her jacket she could see her breasts overflowing from the cups of her bra; the buttons of her blouse strained against their buttonholes. 'Anne Donaghue,' she thought. 'A good, solid name. A policewoman's name.'

But between the two solid buttresses of her name, her confirmation name flittered. How could she have forgotten? She'd chosen it, after all. She felt a hot flush burst over her. Looking around her and, seeing no one, she sank gratefully onto a nearby bench. How could she have picked such a name? It was so floaty and ephemeral. She raked through her memory looking for a scenario to fit this new information.

Anne Donaghue at eleven about to be confirmed. She was remembering now. Yes, Cecilia was definitely the name of a victim. A martyr certainly, that's why she'd picked it.

Nearing adolescence, she'd felt persecuted and misunderstood and the name Cecilia had jumped out at her from the
book of saints and martyrs. Cecilia. Virgin martyr. How
could she have forgotten so completely? What else could she
have forgotten?

In the police station Mrs Dawson was getting agitated.
'Seems to me it's all true about the police these days. All
embezzlement and corruption is it? And no thought for Mr
and Mrs Bryant and them missing for two weeks now. I'd
look into it myself if it wasn't for my health. And their
Cecilia, with the windows wide open and not a thought for
the furniture fading. Father Kelly can deal with her spiritual
welfare of course, but that's not a lot of good to poor Edna.
You've not heard the last of it, I can tell you.'

Cecilia sat on the edge of her father's bed and tried to recall
exactly what had happened. The facts, as the policewoman
called them. Her parents had disappeared without trace. It
had been reported, so they were official missing persons
now. What with WPC Donaghue and the neighbours and
the visitors who might pop in, she didn't want to disappoint
them.

   She imagined her confession, to the policewoman and then
to Father Kelly. She tried to think about what people wanted
from her, how she could please them and balance it with her
own thoughts and what she remembered. After all, in a
proper confession a bad thought was as much a sin as a bad
deed, and she'd had more than her fair share of bad thoughts.
   'Officer, I have to confess. I've committed a terrible

crime. At least I think I have. The more time passes the more it seems certain. It's my parents, you see. I imagined it over and over again until it was perfected. They were drowsy, they'd had their walk and it was late. It was easy enough. I remembered all the sailor's knots that Daddy taught me before; the reef knot and the bowline and the fisherman's bend. And a beautiful new white rope was coiled on the kitchen table, waiting. Waiting to be flung across the garden like a lasso, towards me, to make a new washing line. Only instead of being flung towards me, it was wound around them. I had to gag them quickly. The sound of her voice, grating, berating. I meant them no harm.

'There was a bit of a struggle, of course, but I made them into two neat bundles. Each of those knots were perfect, I could see his eyes checking. Ankles bound together with a surgeon's knot, like a reef knot but stronger. And wrists lightly behind their backs, and great swirls of the rope around and around in a running bowline that tightens up the more you pull it. And finished off at the ends with a fisherman's bend, binding them to the chairs. It made it easier you see, to slide them up the stairs and topple them into the wardrobe. And buried them beneath piles of old fur coats, itching and sneezing and closing their eyes and their mouths against the dust and the stink of mothballs. Then I closed the door on them, slowly and very deliberately, and I turned the key in the lock.

'I pulled over the big leather chair and I was their jailor then. I was their guardian, I knew what was best. I could hear their bumps and muffled pleas of protest but I sat firm. "It's for your own good," I called above the banging.

"You've got to be cruel to be kind." I kept them there for days, throwing in more coats and cushions as each day passed. But I didn't leave them, at least not too long. Long enough for them to sweat and sweat and smoulder and shrink. When I took them out they were tiny. Small as foetuses they were, and the rope had fallen away from them, with the knots, good knots they were, still in place, and limp they were, from the heat. I held them briefly in the palms of my hands.

'In the kitchen I put each of them in a big old kilner jar from the larder and covered the top with greaseproof paper held down with an elastic band. Carefully I pricked the top with a fork as if they were grasshoppers. I carried them carefully, gingerly, into the front room, whispering to reassure them. I put them on the mantelpiece for a while, in place of the china dogs. I felt so fond of them, you can't imagine. So fond of them and a little sad. Poor things, they looked so frail.'

'Pickles and jars, wardrobes and coats.' Perhaps she had told WPC Donaghue already, she couldn't remember now. If she confessed at least she wouldn't have to worry any more about whether it was her fault or not. And the more she went over the details, the more true it seemed. Mrs Dawson was usually right, after all, and Father Kelly was only expressing his concern.

At the station, the Chief Inspector had noticed a change in WPC Donaghue. 'Must have got herself a boyfriend,' he thought. 'But God knows who, she's such a battleship of a girl, and morbid with it.' There was a new looseness about the way she sat and walked, in the way she held herself. She didn't seem so rigid, so held in, and there was almost a dreamy look in her eye. 'Straighten up, Donaghue,' he snapped as she passed. 'Solved the Bryant case, have you?'

In the meadows, at the end of the garden of thirty-two, Acacia Road, clumps of wild thyme grew over the small mounds of earth where the ants live. The Large Blue butterfly has laid her eggs. Her young caterpillars are feeding on the wild thyme and the older caterpillars are living inside the ant-hills, eating the larvae and pupae of the ants. The ants treat the caterpillars with care; they don't harm them, because the caterpillars secrete drops of a special fluid which they find irresistible. The pupae rest among the ants until the emergence of the new Large Blues.

The next time WPC Donaghue called at Cecilia's house, the back door was locked and there was no reply to her knock. Walking back around to the front, she noticed that all the windows and doors were closed. She cupped her eyes against the front window but couldn't see anything through the heavy net. Above a chrysalis that had spun itself into a corner of the frame, she saw that the curtain gaped slightly. Peering inside, the sitting room seemed unchanged except for two jars that stood on the mantelpiece on either side of the sailing ship in a bottle. The gold-edged labels on the front of the jars were neatly inscribed in Roman script, so that they looked like old-fashioned pharmaceutical specimens. Floating upright in some kind of liquid there were what appeared to be dolls. One jar was labelled 'rum' and the doll wore a sailor suit; in the other jar, marked 'holy water', the little female doll was dressed in green.

WPC Donaghue frowned; she didn't remember them at all. She knocked again and waited, before she turned to go. By the door she almost tripped over a bulbous, brown paper package with her name written across it in the same neat Roman script as inscribed the jar labels. With one last glance at the door, she shrugged, picked up the parcel, and departed.

After the policewoman had gone, Cecilia went from room to room, opening all the doors and windows. In the front par-lour the sun shone on to the upholstery and the heavy dark furniture as she pulled the curtains back and opened the win-dows wide. She smiled. 'Fade, fade,' she thought. She spun around in the centre of each room until she felt dizzy and her hair stood out like helicopter blades around her head. She watched the particles of dust caught in the rays of the sun. Out of the corner of her eye she thought she saw bubbles rise in the glass jars on the mantelpiece. She frowned, then moved the jars back into the larder.

In her flat, WPC Donaghue ran a bath before she sat down to open the package and unfold the heavy, almost black, satin kimono. There was a little note from Cecilia pinned to it that said 'Thought you might like this – Cecilia.'

WPC Donaghue felt tears prick in her eyes as she traced the twisted branches of embroidery. No one had ever given her anything pretty before. She laid the kimono on the floor and stretched out the winged sleeves so that it looked as if it was about to take flight. The gold threads of the dragon unravelled across the back.

In the bathroom, she slowly unbuttoned her jacket amidst the steam and, releasing her body from the restrictions of her uniform, let it fall in a heap on the bathroom floor. As she looked down at herself her body seemed to be divided into capsules by folds of flesh and the marks from her uniform. 'Poor, poor Cecilia,' she sighed, as much for a part of herself as for Cecilia Bryant. In the bath, she soaked away the red marks that criss-crossed her body like weals. She was remembering herself at eleven, searching for a new name. She'd chosen Cecilia because Cecilia, with her lute, was the patron saint of musicians, and she'd harboured dreams then of the opera. As she sponged herself she watched the globules of oil floating in the water. She'd wanted to be a second Maria Callas and to fill great halls with her voice. For those short weeks, awaiting confirmation, she'd forgotten she was a Donaghue with a future already laid out. In the bath, her ample mounds of flesh glistened with oil and she looked as voluptuous as a Stone Age goddess.

Afterwards, she paraded around the flat wearing the kimono. She swung her legs over the backs of chairs and sashayed around the settee. Her mother had thought she'd chosen St Cecilia because she was a virgin martyr, and her father because she was stubborn. Hadn't it taken more than three blows of an axe to her neck and an attempted suffocation – and still it took her three days to die? The eleven-year-old Anne had never told them of her dreams; of the Anna Cecilia she might have been. And she'd completely forgotten all about it until her first visit to Acacia Road.

The telephone rang and interrupted her. 'A fire? At number thirty-two. Is Cecilia alright?'

Dusk settled like soot as Anne Cecilia Donaghue ran along Acacia Road. For a moment, in the distance, she thought she saw a pale and white Cecilia rise up on mothy wings above the quiet suburban street, her pale, iridescent wings glittering in the moonlight. Dressed in civilian clothes, Anne Cecilia finally arrived to see number thirty-two engulfed in flames. She could hear the sound of glass jars splintering and bursting in the heat. In the sky above, an archaic Ghost moth, large as a bat, flew amidst the sparks.

In a small but respectable hotel in Eastbourne, an old couple in their seventies were happily settled into their new surroundings. On fluffy pink chairs that matched the counterpane, they sat on either side of the large double bed that dominated the room. The old lady was smiling gleefully over at her husband.

'We've done it,' she said. 'It's more than a month and they haven't found us. And no one here suspects us. After all, we haven't done anything wrong. We've done it, we really have got away. It's just you and me now,' she said as she stroked the pink counterpane fondly.

'Yes, Edna love. I do believe we've got away with it, after all.'

'A walk along the sea front, dear?' she asked.

The couple rose from their chairs simultaneously, and Mr Bryant ceremoniously bowed and crooked his arm. Mrs Bryant giggled as she took his arm and they left the room.

BIOGRAPHICAL NOTES

SYLVIA BROWNRIGG was born in California and grew up there and in Oxford, England. Her fiction has appeared in various American journals, including *Mississippi Review* and *Event*; her journalism in the *Village Voice*, *New York Newsday* and the London *Guardian*. She now lives in London where she is working on a second novel.

MIRIAM BURKE was born and brought up in the west of Ireland. She completed a Ph.D. in Psychology and has worked as a clinical psychologist in the British National Health Service for seventeen years. She started writing fiction in 1995. She lives in London.

SALLY CAMERON was born in Leeds in 1961. She now lives in East London where she divides her time between writing and developing a community garden.

JACQUELYN COLEMAN was born in Tottenham to parents of Jamaican descent. She taught English Language at the comprehensive school where she was taught as a child. She now works with troubled children in London where she lives.

HELENA ECHLIN was born in 1975 in London and attended the Henrietta Barnett school. After a year out, spent working and travelling, she now reads English at Oxford University.

MAGGIE HARRIS was born in Guyana. Her writing has appeared in various anthologies, *Wasafiri* and *Virago New Poets*. She was the winner of the T.S. Eliot Poetry Prize 1994 and was Kent's outstanding Adult Learner in 1994. Her play *Rainstorm* was performed in 1995. Her work as a visual artist has been exhibited in Kent and the Mall Galleries. She lives in Kent.

ALISON MACLEOD is a Canadian now living in West Sussex. At the age of twenty-two, she moved to England to do an MA in Creative Writing at Lancaster University, and is still here, eight years later. Her first novel, *The Changeling* (1996), is published by Macmillan. Her short fiction has won awards in various competitions. Alongside her writing, she lectures in English at the Chichester Institute of Higher Education.

DEBORAH MOFFAT was born in Vermont, USA, in 1953. Her short stories and poems have appeared in a wide variety of periodicals and anthologies, including the *Listener*, *P.N. Review*, *Cosmopolitan*, Faber's *First Fictions* and Bloomsbury's *Soho Square*. She lives in Scotland.

Biographical Notes

CATHY NADEN is a performer and writer living in Sheffield. Since 1984 she has worked with a leading experimental ensemble, Forced Entertainment, touring new performance work widely in this country and abroad. More recently, she has worked for film and radio and is currently studying for an MA in Creative Writing at Sheffield Hallam University.

CHARLOTTE PRICE was born and bred in Greenwich Village, New York. She took an undergraduate degree in Painting and Creative Writing and a Master's in Comparative Literature. She now lives in London, studying fiction-writing at the City Lit. She is currently working on a novel.

SALLY REEVES was born in Hampshire in 1944 and has been writing since childhood. She has had poetry and non-fiction published in magazines. Her particular interest is writing fiction. In 1995 she had to retire from her job as social worker in a hospice through ill health from ME. She lives in Southampton.

MARION URCH was born in England to Irish parents. She is an award-winning video artist. Since 1992 she has been writing full-time. *The Long Road* was broadcast by RTE and won an LBC/GLA Radio Playwrights Award. Her short stories have been published in America and Canada, and her first novel *Violent Shadows* (1996) is published by *Headline Review*. She lives in London.